VIGILANTE LAW

Blue Creek Ben Chisum rescues a homesteader from ruthless vigilantes. The grateful man offers him a half share in his farming business. Ben is loath to become involved in a range war, but accepts after learning that his treacherous old partner, Squint Rizzo, is involved with the vigilantes. But how can one man defeat a ruthless gang of land grabbers? Blue Creek sets out to prove that his reputation for fighting on the side of justice has been well earned.

SPECIAL MESSAGE TO READERS

THE ULVERSCROFT FOUNDATION

(registered UK charity number 264873)

was established in 1972 to provide funds for research, diagnosis and treatment of eye diseases. Examples of major projects funded by the Ulverscroft Foundation are:-

- The Children's Eye Unit at Moorfelds Eye Hospital, London
- The Ulverscroft Children's Eye Unit at Great Ormond Street Hospital for Sick Children
- Funding research into eye diseases and treatment at the Department of Ophthalmology, University of Leicester
- The Ulverscroft Vision Research Group, Institute of Child Health
- Twin operating theatres at the Western Ophthalmic Hospital, London
- The Chair of Ophthalmology at the Royal Australian College of Ophthalmologists

You can help further the work of the Foundation by making a donation or leaving a legacy. Every contribution is gratefully received. If you would like to help support the Foundation or require further information, please contact:

THE ULVERSCROFT FOUNDATION
The Green, Bradgate Road, Anstey
Leicester LE7 7FU, England
Tel: (0116) 236 4325
website: www.ulverscroft-foundation.org.uk

DALE GRAHAM

◆

VIGILANTE LAW

Complete and Unabridged

LINFORD
Leicester

First published in Great Britain in 2018 by
Robert Hale
an imprint of The Crowood Press
Wiltshire

First Linford Edition
published 2021
by arrangement with The Crowood Press
Wiltshire

A catalogue record for this book is available
from the British Library.

ISBN 978–1–4448–4714–7

Published by
Ulverscroft Limited
Anstey, Leicestershire

Printed and bound in Great Britain by
TJ Books Ltd., Padstow, Cornwall

This book is printed on acid-free paper

Author's Note

Throughout the territories west of the Mississippi, few areas managed to escape the blight of vigilante law. This violent affliction held the land in its grip for too long before official justice swept it away. Over two hundred such movements, stretching from Montana in the north to Texas in the south, pitted entrenched and powerful land-owning interests against incoming settlers. The latter had been granted open land under the Homestead Act of 1862 that they were eager to acquire, much to the anger of the existing cattle-owning inhabitants.

The conflict became known as the Western Civil War of Incorporation. Barbed wire and the use of hired gunslingers were paramount in the cattle barons' quest to maintain a firm hold on land viewed as theirs by right of occupancy.

The worst affected state was Montana, where ruthless cattleman Granville

Stuart established the violent ethos of vigilantism to rid the state of insurgents viewed as bandits and rustlers. Adopting the grizzly title of Stuart's Stranglers, the gang ranged far and wide in a brutal campaign. Their burning and killing devastated the land with no hindrance from distant authorities. Indeed, the so-called 'incorporation' was regarded as a legitimate means of establishing law and order.

Further south, in New Mexico, the Lincoln County War of 1878 was made famous by the involvement of Billy the Kid, who took the side of the underdogs. Beef contracts with the army at Fort Stanton, together with the monopoly on local supplies at the general store in Lincoln lay at the heart of the troubles.

When Billy's boss, English rancher John Tunstall, was callously ambushed and shot dead by hired killers brought in by a powerful group of businessmen (known as the House) the Kid, along with fellow Regulators, took their revenge. The Lincoln conflict only lasted five months but it saw the House emerge victorious. This war was fundamental in pitching the Kid into a life of crime that was to end in his suspicious death at the hands of Pat Garrett three years later.

Perhaps the most well known of these range wars was that in Wyoming. Here, a band of Texas gunmen was hired by martinet Major John Walcott to combat the steady influx of squatters and sodbusters occupy-ing the open range. The Johnson County War of 1892 was a classic conflict between a self-seeking powerful faction and the small settler who only wanted to work land legitimately granted by government decree.

When the settlers innocently appropriated unbranded calves found wandering the range, a maverick law was passed by the Cattlemen's Association, which made the practice illegal. Every so-called rustler caught netted the hired gunman $250. Frank Canton, the leader of these so-called 'range detectives', made a good living from this dubious law. Communications with the outside world had been cut off. Wyoming was now isolated and alone. The stage was all set for a clearance, cattle baron style.

Small settlers were threatened with summary removal if they did not surrender and leave the territory. Lynchings and shootings of those who resisted the takeovers became commonplace. Most famous was that of Nate Champion, who left a written account of his resistance. But it was to no avail. Following a lone and spirited defence, he was shot down while trying to flee a burning cabin. This heinous misdeed caused uproar among the local citizenry, who formed a resistance movement of their own.

Walcott and his Regulators were trapped in a barn on the TA ranch south of the town of Buffalo. Total annihilation was threatened. Bloodshed was only averted by the timely arrival of the cavalry from Fort McKinney. It is perhaps inevitable under the political system of the time that conviction of Walcott, Canton and the other invaders failed. But Nate Champion, a simple cowboy caught up in the brutal conflict, lived up to his name by becoming a revered folk hero.

Granville Stuart, Frank Canton and Billy the Kid have passed down into Western history as the most notable participants in the cattle versus nester range wars. But there were other gunslingers that made their mark in the menacing upsurge of vigilante law.

Although Ben Chisum never featured in the annals of Texas history, his contribution to the establishment of law and order in the border territories will long be remembered. Folk still talk of the vital role the man they called Blue Creek played in defusing the havoc caused by land-hungry desperadoes.

This is his story.

1

Dancing with the Devil

For upwards of a week, Ben Chisum had been trekking on foot across the desolate wasteland of southwest Texas. Disaster struck when his horse stepped in a gopher hole and broke its leg soon after crossing the deep ravine cut by the mighty Rio Grande at Eagle Pass. Elation at crossing the border between Mexico and the United States was suddenly stymied. Having to put a bullet through the poor critter's brain was the only answer. The animal's demise hit the man hard. They had been together four years.

He carried the saddle on his back for the next three days, hoping to come across some place where he could obtain a fresh mount. Not a single soul was encountered. Tired and footsore, Ben was forced to abandon it, covering the highly prized Mexican saddle with brushwood until such time as it could be recovered.

Stops for rest were becoming ever more frequent. On the eighth day he lay down in the shade of a clump of cottonwoods. The sleep of exhaustion claimed his body. It was some time later that an alien sound dragged him out of the clammy hands of Morpheus. He raised a weary frame up onto one elbow and shook the mush from his head. Something had awakened him. Ears pricked up to the prattle of human voices! And they were coming from the far side of the copse.

At long last he had come across people. Surely he would now be able to hire, buy or borrow a horse to continue his journey. On listening some more, Ben realized that this was no light-hearted banter between friends. Anger was clearly at the heart of the verbal exchange. A slow crawl across open ground found the covert traveller secreted behind a pile of fallen tree trunks. He peeked around the edge, anxious not to reveal his presence until the source of the flinty altercation had been determined.

Bulging peepers were now witness to an ugly sight. Some poor jasper with hands tied behind his back and straddling a mustang was being berated by a burly critter. Noticeable was the livid scar warping the assailant's leathery features from mouth to ear.

The disfigurement had resulted from a knife slash delivered by a Comanche brave. The irate Indian had objected to his sister being molested by a hated white eye. Web Steiger had discovered the squaw alone, washing her hair in a creek during a cattle drive on the Western Trail heading for Dodge City. Escape was only achieved when his partner gunned the skunk down. Unfortunately, the gunfire had attracted the rest of the raiding party, forcing the duo to flee for their lives.

Following that unsavoury incident, they had been forced to abandon the drive and go on the prod. The clash had left Steiger with an abiding hatred of all things Indian. In his eyes, an inherited blend of Mex and white was little better. Accordingly, the target of the gang leader's abhorrence could expect no quarter.

The watcher couldn't help noting the bruised and bloody face of the tethered half-breed. The poor sap had clearly been roughed up severely prior to his current predicament. Upwards of a dozen onlookers surrounded the object of their sickening aggression. None of the pitiless faces bore any hint of sympathy for their victim.

The boss man slipped a noosed rope over the guy's head and then tossed the slack end over a sturdy branch. 'This is what happens to rustlers in the Nueces Valley.' The snarled words of the gang leader were distinct and unambiguous. 'Branding calves by sodbusters on open range has been made illegal. And you're gonna pay the full price.' Murmurs of agreement rippled through the ugly gathering.

'You're a trespasser with no right to that land.'

'I've as much right to occupy it as

4

anybody else. More than a skunk like you, that's for darned sure,' the captive, whose name was Chico Lafferty, spat out. If'n these varmints figured he was gonna beg for mercy, they could go piss into the wind. 'I've worked it for danged near five years under the government's Homestead Act. One hundred and sixty acres of open land. That's what it says and you ain't got no right to muscle in.'

Although Ben was unable to assist the man, he couldn't help but respect his gutsy resolve. Ben's fists bunched in anger. Yet much as he yearned to jump out and challenge these bushwhackers, he knew it would be a sure-fire suicidal decision. All he could do was bide his time and hope for a slice of luck to come his way.

The leader of the hunting pack responded with a growled stream of pro-fane curses, lashing out with a vicious backhander. Only the tautness of the rope saved the nester from tumbling out of the saddle. 'This rope says I got every right. There ain't no official law down here in south Texas except what we make ourselves.'

'This ain't proper law. You scum are nought but a bunch of stinking vigilantes out for your own ends.' Lafferty was scared for his well-being, but a lifetime of struggling against the taint of being mixed-race, not to mention the harsh landscape, bolstered his courage. A globule of sputum splattered across the braggart's face. 'Do your worst, Steiger. Justice and fair play will out in the end, and then it'll be you and your kind dancing with the Devil.'

A mirthless grin of accord cracked the watcher's weathered face. *You show these yellow skunks they can't grind you down, old-timer.* Yet he knew it was an impotent avowal of support. The end was only moments away as the incensed leader scraped the goo from his face angrily.

The insulting denigration by the tethered 'breed was the last straw for the enraged vigilante. 'We were gonna make it quick, jerking you to Jesus. No chance of that now. It's gonna be a slow one for you, 'breed. And while you're a-choking on the end of that rope, think well on what a stubborn unwillingness to accept progress has brought down on your miserable head. You should have left while you had the chance. Too late now.'

Like a white worm, the knife scar appeared to writhe on the killer's face. 'OK, Buckshot, pull that cayuse from under the critter,' he ordered a subordinate. 'And make it nice and slow; I want to see this dung beetle performing for Old Nick.'

Hollers of delight followed as the victim was launched into space. A brief moment of cold-hearted pleasure was all Web Steiger could afford to admire his handiwork. Too much time had been spent already exchanging insults with this critter. There were other fish to fry. If things went to plan, another few weeks would see the whole of the Nueces Valley in his hands.

'OK boys, let's go,' he ordered his men. 'We got us a meet with another turnip down yonder who needs our expert assistance.' Ugly guffaws all round greeted this piece of grizzly wit as the gang spurred off, leaving their victim desperately kicking his life out.

Before the riders were even out of sight, the witness to this heinous crime emerged from cover and dashed across the open ground. Already, the feeble struggle for life was fast disappearing. Would he be in time to save the guy? Extracting a knife from a belt sheath, he slashed at the thick hemp. The victim hit the ground like a sack of corncobs and lay still.

A quick check registered a thin pulse in the man's lacerated neck. At least he was still in the land of the living. But for how long? Water from a canteen was dribbled between purple lips, eliciting a bout of coughing as the man slowly opened his eyes. 'Take it easy, mister,' his saviour advised, wiping the blooded face with a bandanna before carefully removing the stiff necktie. 'Another minute and you'd have been strumming with the angels.'

The man winced as a searching finger traced a path across the rough laceration encircling his neck. A watery eye lifted to his redeemer. 'Wh-who do I have to th-thank for saving me?' he croaked out.

'The name is Ben Chisum,' was the quiet response as he eased the man into a sitting position. 'Some folks call me Blue Creek.'

The name certainly struck home, stirring some life into the flickering regard. Lafferty nodded. 'Guess I should have recognized you from those rattler tailbones in your hatband. I heard tell you were over the border in Zaragoza helping the revolutionaries. What in thunder you doing up here in the Nueces?'

'I had me some trouble,' was the studied reply. No elaboration was forthcoming. 'Needed to shift my ass in a hurry when things got a tad hairy.'

Lafferty did not delve any further. A man's business was his own affair. 'Well, it's my good fortune you happened along.' But he did have one query.

'This ain't the best country to be cast afoot, though.'

'My horse broke a leg. I had to shoot

the poor critter.' He helped the badly shaken homesteader into a more comfortable position. 'That was a week back. I been on the hoof ever since. Ain't met a soul until now. Hearing those voices was music to my ears until I realized what they were doing.'

The man held out a weathered hand, which Ben accepted. 'The name is Chico Lafferty. I run a spread at the bottom end of the valley called the Jaybird. It's on good land with a regular water supply for the crops. I run a few cattle for milk but the grass is too sparse. It certainly ain't ranching country. They accused me of rustling, which is a danged lie. I bought those steers fair and square.'

'So why is the guy so keen to grab your land?'

'Can't figure it out. He's a cattleman through and through. Farming sure ain't his game.' Angry resentment at the brutal treatment meted out by the gang creased him up. His throat felt like it was on fire. Ben dribbled more water down the parched gullet and waited until the guy was ready to continue.

'My figuring is he hates nesters coming in and farming the land and just wants the whole valley for himself. He's been putting the squeeze on others to leave. Anybody refuses and this is what happens to them.' Again, he gingerly felt the sore abrasion around his neck. 'I'd have gone the same way if'n you hadn't moseyed by.'

'Who's running this murdering crew?' Ben asked.

'The leader is Web Steiger. He's the jasper sporting that ugly snake on his kisser. A real mean cuss if ever there was one.' Lafferty's eyes glittered with heated malice. 'He won't accept the government ruling that this is open land for anyone to farm. There's enough room here for everyone. But as you've seen, he'll go to any lengths to force us all out. Calls himself a vigilante chief, claiming we're rustlers and horse thieves and that he's only trying to establish law and order.'

'Can't the local tin star curb his aggression?' Ben asked.

Lafferty shrugged resignedly. 'That's the trouble. We ain't gotten no official law in this part of Texas yet. And until we have, his warped version of land management can't be challenged.'

'Looks like I seem to have stumbled into a range war,' Ben mused. His reserved manner hinted that he was decidedly reticent about becoming involved. 'If'n we ride double and head for the nearest town, I could buy me a fresh horse and light out of here.'

'Hold on there, *compadre*,' Lafferty said, laying a restraining hand on his rescuer's arm. 'That don't seem the right course of action for a *hombre* with your reputation.'

'And what might that be?' Chisum's response was cautious, reserved.

'Everybody knows how Blue Creek Ben Chisum single-handedly cleaned up San Angelo and Val Verde.' The sodbuster's eyes glittered with enthusiasm as he continued pouring out praise onto his liberator. 'You're a man who stands up to injustice, fights for those who only want what's rightfully theirs. Ain't that why you were down in Zaragoza?' He didn't wait for a response. 'The good folks round here need a saviour like you to stand up to Web Steiger and his gang.'

A diffident hand waved away the effusive praise for his gun-toting actions up north. 'You're right about Val Verde,' he said, lifting a wary eyebrow. 'But even the great Ben Chisum needed some help with those bad boys in San Angelo.' A dark shadow clouded his features as recall of that help resurrected bad memories.

The farmer did not notice the sudden cooling of his liberator's mood. 'Just goes to prove what I said,'

Lafferty persisted. 'You're the man to hogtie these galoots and bring peace back to the Nueces.'

Ben was not convinced. He'd had enough of other people's troubles. The fiasco over the border in Zaragoza had left a bad taste in his mouth. Due to the backstabbing betrayal of a partner he had trusted, six hard months had been spent in a Mexican jail. And during all that time, he was left to languish on death row whilst never knowing when the proverbial axe would fall. The experience was enough to curb anybody's appetite for adventure. He needed to rest up before again selling his gun to settle any other reckless insurrection.

'I don't know, Chico,' Ben hesitated.

But Lafferty was not giving in that easily. 'This latest attack by Steiger has left me exposed. And I ain't afraid to admit that I'm scared. There's no legal document to prove this land is mine. Never felt the need for it before. So anybody strong enough can take it over. And I can't do a darned thing to stop them.' The urgency of the farmer's entreaty had taken a lot out of him. His gravelly voice stumbled to a series of rasping grunts. He fell back, exhausted, as the near-death experience reasserted its debilitating consequences.

'Not so fast, old-timer,' Ben reproved gently. 'You need a doctor to check you out. Dancing with the Devil ain't good for the body, nor the soul.'

Lafferty rallied quickly. He ignored the advice, continuing with his petition. 'Forget all that. This is more important. I can write a letter for you to instruct a lawyer I know to draw up an agreement. It'll make you a legally binding partner in the Jaybird. All you have to do then is lodge it at the bank in Uvalde. State-sanctioned endorsement will curb Steiger's foul ambitions. Even he ain't foolish enough to think he can take over an officially-endorsed property.'

Ben was still not convinced. 'You sure about this? You don't even know me.'

Lafferty waved away the uncertainty. 'That reputation for doing good deeds is more than enough to convince me you're the man to help me out.' Thoroughly enthused, the guy struggled to his feet. 'Us small guys badly need help if'n we're to survive. And you'll be well paid. I'll make sure of it. You're gonna need supplies to run the place.'

Ben's shoulders lifted to indicate he was stony broke. 'All I have is the clothes on my back and a few sticks of jerky.'

Lafferty fished out a billfold hidden under his saddle and pealed off a wad of greenbacks. 'Those critters searched me, but failed to find this.' He chuckled at the recollection. 'Like I said, the Jaybird is a successful farm. This should see you right until we meet up again.'

It sounded a good deal. Yet still Ben hesitated to accept the handout. Would he be exposing himself to a heap of danger he could well do without? It was like putting his head into a snake's nest. Was he ready to take on a ruthless gang of desperadoes with only a reputation and a six-shooter for support? He was just a man alone, and Steiger clearly had a small army at his beck and call.

Lafferty could see the hesitation in his saviour's tightly knit features. The homesteader eyed his associate, willing him desperately to accept the offer. 'And when you've harvested the next crop, we'll split the profits down the middle. Can't say fairer than that. So, what do you say?' He pressed home his offer by a further declaration. 'With you in charge, Steiger will think twice about taking on that gunslinger to back his play.'

Mention of a hired mercenary piqued Ben's curiosity. 'Who has he brought in?' he enquired.

'A real tough *hombre* called Squint Rizzo. Some'n wrong with one eye, but it sure hasn't affected his gun hand. He shot and killed my best pal last week just for looking at him the wrong way.' The farmer's scowled recollection made him miss the sudden interest the name had generated.

'So that backstabbing varmint has decided to join the vigilantes,' Ben muttered under his breath. His presence in Texas changed everything. Squint Rizzo had been his partner down in Zaragoza. It was that Judas who had betrayed Ben to the *federales*, and no doubt for a sight more than thirty pieces of silver.

Ben's silence and muttered imprecation caught the nester's attention. 'You know this fella?'

'You could say,' was the stilted reply,

as Ben Chisum's thoughts veered back to that vindictive betrayal of a once powerful alliance between the two buddies.

2

Sold Down the River

The two men had first met up in New Mexico in the border town of Columbus. Ben had arrived at a critical moment. That had been three years back. But he could still recall the incident as if it had been yesterday. The main street was devoid of activity. Not a soul could be seen. Nothing moved. Not even the twitter of a bird disturbed the macabre silence that reigned supreme.

The newcomer hauled rein, his brow furrowed in puzzlement. A tense atmosphere hung in the fetid air; it was so palpable you could have cut it with a knife. A collective holding of breath had gripped the place. Something was clearly about to happen. Ben drew his horse to one side in time to witness a tall, bronzed figure step out from an alleyway and position himself in the middle of the empty street.

The man's challenge echoed back from the white washed adobe buildings lining both sides of the thoroughfare. 'Guess who has come to town, Tulsa Jake. It's your old buddy, Squint Rizzo. And I'm here to call you out. Just you and me: face-to-face. Let's see if'n all that bluster you been spouting about taking me down is just a load of hot air.'

Tulsa Jake Tralee was a rustler who had been terrorizing the local ranchers with impunity for months. After snatching the cattle, all he had to do was just push them across the border for sale in old Mexico: a simple operation with no danger from over-stretched law enforcement agencies. To counter the outlaw's depredations, the local ranchers had brought in a hired gunslinger to solve the thorn in their side once and for all.

Ben had never come into contact with the hired gunfighter, but he knew of his reputation, and he was curious to witness the outcome of this classic duel in the sun.

Based in Alamagordo, Squint Rizzo

had come highly recommended. Clad in a black leather vest, with black corduroy trousers tucked into a pair of shiny black boots, the gunman presented a formidable image. The tough persona was intended to strike fear into his adversaries. The wayward eye causing a permanent leer only served to enhance the intimidating aura surrounding the man. And it had clearly worked its magic on the local townsfolk. As to whether Jake Tralee would be similarly cowed, now that was another matter.

Ben watched the all-too-familiar scene unfold with interest. He had been in a similar position on numerous occasions himself. But one hired gunfighter studying the tactics of another was a rare occurrence. Ben felt strangely privileged for such a situation to have presented itself, and he was thoroughly intrigued to see how his opposite number would deal with the renowned outlaw. Tulsa Jake was worth a cool thousand bucks, dead or alive.

Rizzo had checked his double-holstered

gun rig. The right-hand Colt Frontier was tied down in the standard way with the left for emergencies in cross-draw mode. Ben nodded to himself — impressive! This guy appeared to know his stuff. But how would he perform under pressure? The gunman stood there, alone, hands flexing but with a casual demeanour essential for a rapid action response when the imminent conflict blew up.

Ben crossed his arms, leaning against the side of a fence. Out of sight, he still had a good view of the upcoming gladiatorial combat. An expectant half-smile creased the handsome profile. If Rizzo failed to remove Jake Tralee, the path would be open for him to assess what went wrong and step into the empty void. A thousand dollar reward was not to be sniffed at.

His back stiffened as Tulsa Jake emerged from the gloomy confines of the Blind Owl saloon. An unlit cigar was stuck between his teeth. A black beard encased a face riven by a lifetime of lawless endeavour. The man's cold appraisal of his challenger held no fear as he leaned casually against a veranda post. 'Figure you can take old Tulsa out, mister?' The question was chock full of disdain. 'Others have tried. And as you can see, they've all failed. You ain't gonna be any luckier.'

'You're all talk and no action, Jake,' came back the scornful reply, as Rizzo removed a watch from his vest pocket and laid it on a barrel. 'When the music stops, we get to shooting.' He flipped a lever and a mellifluous series of notes, sinuous yet hauntingly beautiful, filled the air.

A full minute passed as the melody slowly wound down. Ben's focussed gaze shifted between the two men. If anything, Tulsa Jake seemed the more at ease. He'd heard tales of Squint Rizzo's defective vision being no hindrance to his gun hand. Did Tralee reckon to be faster?

Moments before the music faded, Ben discovered the answer to the conundrum. A movement over to his right found him eyeballing a hidden bushwhacker.

Where there was one, others would be close by. Rapid panning of the immediate surroundings revealed another up on the roof of the general store and yet another behind a wagon over on the far side of the street. Little wonder that the owlhoot was unfazed by the challenger.

A clear-cut shootout was one thing. But dry-gulching was the action of a coward, and the lowest form of life. Drawing his own single-action Colt .45, Ben called out a stark warning. 'It's a set-up, Rizzo. Two bushwhackers on your right. I'll handle the other rat.' Surprise registered on the gunman's face. Yet, ever the professional, he ducked down on one knee. A hawkish gaze swept the street, searching out the hidden assailants.

In the flick of a gnat's wing, gunfire erupted. Caught out by this sudden and unexpected thwarting of his underhanded chicanery, Tulsa Jake was the first to fall victim to the newcomer's timely intervention. The prospect of an easy removal of the hired gunman had made him careless. The error ended with his own removal from this mortal coil.

The surprise ambush was now turned on its head. Panic had gripped the hidden assassins. As a result, shooting from the two ambushers at ground level was wild and uncontrolled, giving Rizzo time to eyeball the skunks and remove them from the affray.

Only the man on the roof of the store remained a threat. He had a rifle that was now used to deadly effect. Caught out in the open, Rizzo took a bullet in the leg. He went down, but still managed to crawl behind a water trough as more bullets kicked up dust around him.

'Stay where you are,' Ben called out. 'I'll flush the critter out.' Tendrils of curling gun smoke drifting across the field of battle enabled him to scurry unseen across to the far side of the street. There he slipped down a narrow passage, circling around to locate the building where the dry-gulcher was secreted.

A couple of barrels enabled him to scramble up onto the back of the roof. Peering over the edge, he could see a crouched figure hiding behind a chimney. His whole attention was concentrated on the main street. Ben levered himself up quietly onto the sloping roof and slowly edged across to catch the sniper unawares. His luck failed when a loose slat creaked beneath his boot.

Instantly sentient to the presence of danger, the man swung round, pointing his rifle. He was no slouch and managed to trigger off a shot, but too fast. It missed by a whisker, burning a hole in Ben's hat and rattling the ghoulish keepsake. Levering a second shell into the upper chamber of the Winchester allowed Ben sufficient time to place his own reply, dead centre. A red splash blossomed on the man's chest: a killing shot. He fell back, disappearing over the edge of the roof. Moments later a dull thud heralded a meeting with the hard ground below.

Another unseen assailant, crouching in an alleyway on the far side of the street, had clearly adjudged the ambush to be a lost cause. Moments later, he dashed out on his horse, frantically leathering the animal to the gallop. The intended escape was cut short abruptly when Ben snatched up the fallen Winchester and pumped a couple of shots his way. Both were well placed; the rider threw up his arms and tumbled out of the saddle.

Ben then scrambled down off the roof. Still wary that more such miscreants might be hovering in the shadows, he ducked down and waited for any alien response. Only the slow creak of a swinging sign-board disturbed the silence. Satisfied that the brief mêlée was over, he hurried across to check both men had indeed gone to join their buddies stoking up the fiery furnace.

A couple of curious mutts slunk across to sniff at one of the corpses littering the street. They were followed by a few more curious creatures of the two-legged variety. With the infamous rustler and his gang no longer a threat, fear had taken a back seat.

'You alright over there?' Ben called to his fellow protection specialist. A blood-smeared hand raised above the trough told him that Rizzo was still in the land of the living. But he was clearly hurt and in need of a sawbones' proficiency. Still not ready to assume everything was safe, Ben issued a salutary caution. 'Keep your eyes peeled and cover me while I cross the street.'

Moments later, he reached the far side and was helping the injured man to his feet. 'Lucky for me you came along at the right moment, mister, else I'd have been taking up early residence on Boot Hill.'

Rizzo grunted, wincing as Ben tied his bandanna around a blood-smeared leg to staunch the flow. The injured man laid a reflective eye on his benefactor. 'You seem kind of familiar. Have we met before some place?'

Ben shook his head. 'Don't reckon so. But in your case, the funereal gear kind of gives the game away. Not to mention that lopsided look.' He held out a hand, which the man grasped. 'In my game, Squint Rizzo might well be a rival for the best paying jobs.'

'Now I remember.' The wayward peeper flickered. 'Saw your picture in the *South Texas Sentinel*. That was some job you pulled, cleaning up Val Verde of those Mex *bandidos*. Guess I'm now beholden to you, Chisum.'

'Just doing my professional duty, helping a fellow protectionist.' A wry smirk creased Ben's face. 'Although, if truth be told, you were a mite too trusting in figuring a skunk like Tulsa Jake would play by the rules.'

'Guess you're right there, Blue. I owe you a drink for that.'

Ben laid a poignant eye on his associate. 'A bit more than that, I'd say. Reckon this earns me a half share of that reward money, don't you?'

Rizzo's half scowl balked at such a suggestion. This was something he had not considered. But the brittle regard aimed his way curbed any animosity; after all, this guy had saved his life. He nodded. 'Reckon that's a fair deal.'

With the business side of things agreed, it was down to more immediate needs.

'Best we get you serviced by the croaker first,' Ben advised, signalling to a couple of onlookers. A firm voice ordered them to carry Rizzo down to the surgery. No protest was offered. Gunslingers possessed a certain aura that precluded any refusal. Guys of their standing said 'jump', and folks tended to ask 'which way?'

'I'll be in the Blind Owl when you're ready to buy me that drink,' Ben called out, receiving a thumbs-up in return. 'And don't forget to bring the dough.'

The two had become partners. Both figured it was better to join forces and split the proceeds rather than act alone as rivals. The collaboration had worked to their mutual advantage for two years until the green-eyed monster had reared its ugly head. Money talks where hired gunmen are concerned. And Squint Rizzo lacked the scruples of fair play that his associate took for granted. The climax of their brief liaison came to a brutal finale in Zaragoza.

That was where the trust Ben Chisum had unwittingly placed in his partner's hands was ignored callously. And all for what? He shuddered at the recollection — what else but money, US dollars?

The Mexican *federales* had the resources to pay far more than cash-strapped *peons* struggling to secure a decent life for themselves and their families. Unlike his avaricious partner, Ben had refused to sell them down the river. As such, it was he who was duped by the proverbial dousing.

Rizzo had secretly informed the authorities about the location of their campsite. The skunk had made an excuse about visiting a nearby cantina for some female companionship. That had left the trail wide open for a night time ambush. It was in the early hours when the peace had been shattered by shouts and gunfire. Ben hadn't stood a chance. Following his arrest, the *jefe de policia* in charge of the detail had been more than happy to reveal the name of his informant. A trial had followed but the result was a foregone conclusion. Blue Creek Ben Chisum was well known to the authorities, and they were cock-a-hoop to have him under lock and key, secure in a filthy jail cell and a future date with the firing squad.

Months had passed with the threat hanging over him, until the dreaded day finally arrived. The night before the execution, Ben had been fastened to a post in the yard behind the *comisaria* — a warning to all the other prisoners as to the result of insurrection against the state. And there he was left to contemplate his fate on the morrow. What they had failed to do was post a guard. Neither had the authorities reckoned with the esteem in which Blue Creek was held by the downtrodden masses.

Waiting for the moon to slip behind a belt of cloud, shadowy figures then scrambled silently over the enclosing walls. Within minutes the prisoner had been released and spirited away. The grateful rescuers had given him food and weapons. Even his revered horse was saddled and ready for a swift flight across the border.

★ ★ ★

The unsettling recollection had taken but a moment to flit through Ben's mind. But Lafferty was quick to perceive the disturbed aspect troubling his saviour. It was clear that bad blood existed between him and Steiger's recently hired gunnie. 'That skunk must have hurt you something bad,' the homesteader observed. 'Ain't that reason enough for you to accept my proposition?'

The assertion swung Ben's thoughts back to the current situation into which he had lumbered unwittingly. Disclosure of the renegade's presence in the Nueces Valley had certainly piqued his interest. More than that, it was a firm decider. If Squint Rizzo was involved in this conflict, then what sort of craven milksop would Ben Chisum be to walk away? He held out a hand. 'Guess you've gotten yourself a deal, Chico.'

A couple of prairie dogs yipped and scampered about in gleeful accord with the decision. 'Lookee there, *amigo*!' Lafferty pointed to the cavorting duo. 'Even the local wildlife reckons you're the hombre to shackle these *malos* and send them packing.'

His excitement soon simmered down as a pragmatic mind reasserted itself. 'First off, though, you're gonna need help. Go visit with Amos Durham,' Lafferty declared. 'He runs a small spread near Maverick to the south of here. Amos is good with figures and keeps my books up to date. He can show you that the Jaybird is a going concern. I'd trust that guy with my life. So listen up good to what he has to tell you about running the place.'

Lafferty then extracted a scrap of paper and a stubby pencil from his saddle-bag. A brief letter was composed, explaining his proposition. Both men signed it. 'There's a guy in Del Rio who can draw up a binding contract. Then make sure you lodge it in the bank vault at Uvalde.

Emile Santo is a cousin of mine. He's the only man in the territory I'd trust to hold such an important document safely. That'll give Steiger something to brood on.' Lafferty then mounted up. He extended a hand for Ben to join him.

'Won't you be helping out?' Ben asked as he climbed up behind his new partner. 'I'm a bit green when it comes to sodbusting.'

'I'm going into hiding until this business is over.'Lafferty's voice registered fear as he continued. 'Getting your neck stretched and staring the grim reaper in the eye ain't good for the *corazon*.' He tapped his chest. 'Don't mind admitting it's shaken me down to the core. Durham can offer you all the help you need.'

'So where you figuring to go?' Ben posed the question as the lone horse with its double passenger load trotted away from the grim scene of the recent hanging. Ben's eyes scanned the rolling terrain constantly for signs of the perpetrators as he awaited the answer.

'If by any chance you need to communicate with me in a hurry, I have a cousin near Del Rio who'll take me in until it's safe to come out of hiding.'

3

The Blue Creek Bite

They reached the town of Del Rio the following day. A brisk handshake sealed the agreement and the two unlikely associates parted company. 'Good luck to you, Blue Creek. Not that I have any doubts a *hombre* of your standing will send that rat crawling back into the hole he came out of. But remember what I said about taking advice from Amos Durham.'

After presenting the signed instruction to a lawyer, the official business was soon concluded. Anxious not to be eyeballed now that he was in possession of a valuable document, the new partner in Jaybird Holdings was anxious to leave Del Rio behind. Yet, once again, Ben found himself alone and on foot. As a result, his first priority was to hire a buggy and go pick up that prize saddle. Luckily, it was no more than an hour's ride to the south.

After returning the buggy and obtaining a fresh mount, he headed back to the Nueces Valley and the town of Maverick. As suggested by his new partner, the main priority was to find Amos Durham. Sitting astride the sturdy chestnut mare, Ben was idling his way along the town's main street, wondering how best to locate the mysterious homesteader. He kept his head down, hat pulled low over his eyes. For a guy in his profession, it always paid to be cautious. He'd made too many enemies to take life for granted.

Maverick was a typical sleepy town characteristic of south Texas. Most of the buildings were of adobe construction. More recent erections were built in the American style with ornate false fronts. One structure that was notably missing, however, was a sheriff's office. In its place was a sign that read *Office of the Maverick Vigilance Committee. President: Web Steiger*. Ben frowned. It appeared that vigilante law dispensed by Steiger was well established in the Nueces. He was right to be wary having entered the rattler's lair. There was no telling who was friend or foe.

Mexicans, with their distinctive apparel and wearing wide-brimmed sombreros, mingled with Stetson-clad cowboys and homesteaders. Having no idea who could be trusted, Ben considered it wise to treat them all with cagey suspicion.

A couple of jaspers about to cross the street paused to eyeball the stranger in town. Nothing out of the ordinary there, but this newcomer was far from that. Ben Chisum possessed a natural bearing, a certain potent charisma that drew attention. Much as he tried to blend into the landscape, his rangy frame precluded any meaningful anonymity.

He stopped in front of the watching pair. 'I'm looking for a man by the name of Amos Durham. You know where I can find him?'

The taller of the two, a shifty-eyed hard case going under the handle of Laredo pointed down the street absently. His cold regard gave nothing away, just like the deadpan reply. 'You'll likely find him taking a well-earned rest in his favourite spot on the outside of town.'

'Just keep following your nose, mister,' the other man added, unsuccessfully trying to conceal a derisory smirk. 'He'll be on the far side of the church. Poor old Amos ain't much of a talker though.' The two men guffawed in approval of the one-sided comment.

'Much obliged,' Ben replied rather uneasily, not deigning to question the somewhat cavalier remarks as he nudged the chestnut forward. They didn't quite sit right, and left a funny taste in the mouth. He shrugged off the unsettling notion. Doubtless he would find out soon enough if those two idlers were just having fun at a newcomer's expense.

Quizzical looks laced with suspicion prodded the back of the disappearing gunslinger. 'Got me a notion I've seen that critter someplace before,' remarked Laredo, tugging at his lank crop of greasy black hair. 'And I'm figuring him being here ain't gonna be good news.'

40

'You figure we ought to tell the boss?' enquired Bug Pincher, scratching his sides. It was a reluctance to take a bath that found the stocky jigger being thus labelled. Not one to take offence, Pincher had accepted the handle readily, judging it to be a badge of esteem. Guys with nicknames harboured respect. In truth, the opposite was the case. But Ike Pincher was too thick-skinned, or stupid, to know the difference. 'He said for us to report any strangers arriving in the valley. And that guy sure ain't no drifting cowpoke. He could be here to cause trouble.'

His buddy's incidental observation had struck a cord in Laredo's acute memory box. It was that tied-down gun rig that marked him down as a gunslinger. But there was one other more poignant accessory that had clinched the recall, namely the rattler tail in his hatband. 'Geez, I heard that guy was down in Zaragoza helping the revolutionaries. What in tarnation is he doing up here?' A sheen of sweat had broken out on the tough's face.

Bug looked at him askance. He had never had the dubious pleasure of an introduction. 'Who is he?'

Laredo ignored the question while musing on this disquieting development. Ben Chisum here in the Nueces. 'Now, what darned game are you playing, mister? You ain't here on vacation, that's for sure.'

Pincher tugged at his pal's arm, insistent that he be apprised of the mysterious newcomer's identity. 'Come on, Laredo,' he pressed. 'Who the hell is this turkey that's gotten you in such a lather?'

'That, old buddy, is Ben Chisum.'

Pincher's startled expression indicated his knowledge of the man and his reputation. 'You sure about that?' he shot back.

'Ain't I just,' was the caustic rejoinder. 'I was in Blue Creek, Colorado when he took down Wild Johnny Bullstrode. Just walked down the middle of the street, cool as you please, and slugged him with a hard left to the chin before frog-marching him over to the jailhouse. And not a shot fired. Nobody lifted a finger to stop him. It's a new sport they call boxing.' Respect, tinged with a handsome dollop of fear, was clearly evident in Laredo's discourse. 'Never seen anything the like before or since. That guy has got nerves of steel. And now he's here in the Nueces.'

He indicated for his associate to go get their horses. They needed to follow the guy and see what he wanted with Amos Durham.

A quarter-mile beyond the church, Ben came across a group of mourners emerging from the cemetery. They walked towards him slowly. 'I'm looking for a man called Amos Durham,' he asked.

'Well, you're too late, mister,' replied a stocky man, clad in a dark suit that had seen better days. 'We just buried him.'

A young woman stepped forward. She was wiping tears from her face. Even though Elsa Durham was dressed in sepulchral black, there was no denying an attractive female lay beneath. 'What do you want with my father?' she snapped at the newcomer. Her cold gaze rested on the low-slung gun rig. 'If'n you've come to make sure the job was carried out properly, then you're too late.' The woman's caustic retort made no effort to conceal her angry suspicion at this unwanted stranger's presence. 'It was a gunslinger who shot him dead on the veranda of his own house.'

'Was his name by any chance Squint Rizzo?' Ben enquired.

Elsa stiffened. 'He a friend of your'n? Another hired killer?'

Ben quickly held up a conciliatory hand. 'You got me all wrong, ma'am,' he said in an effort to calm things down. The burgeoning storm cloud made her even more alluring than he had previously noticed. 'Rizzo sure ain't no buddy of mine. The exact opposite, if anything.' The bitter riposte certainly caught the distressed girl's attention. Not wishing to antagonize her, he immediately moderated his tone. 'I'm sorry for your loss. But I'm here on the advice of Chico Lafferty. It was him that told me your

44

father could acquaint me with the trouble brewing in these parts.'

'That's a darned lie,' rasped an older man stepping up. Obediah Crawley was the local blacksmith in Uvalde and leader of the town council. Not that he had much power now that Steiger had taken over. 'We have it on good authority the poor guy was hanged by Web Steiger and his bunch of killers.'

Ben sighed. 'And I suppose it was Steiger who told you.' He didn't wait for a confirmation. 'Well, I'm here to set the record straight.' He leaned over the neck of his horse. 'Lafferty is still around, although he's mighty shaken up. Getting your neck stretched is apt to do that to a man. So he's gone into hiding until this shebang blows over.'

'And how do you know all this?' Crawley interjected tersely, still not convinced this stranger was on the level.

Elsa stepped in front of him. 'Was it you that rescued him?' the chastened younger woman enquired, her previous stiff attitude visibly softening towards

45

this enigmatic stranger.

Ben nodded, shifting his gaze back to Elsa Durham. 'And he's put me in charge of his holding. It's been officially certified and sealed by a lawyer in Del Rio. All I gotta do now is deliver it to the bank in Uvalde for safekeeping.'

'You surely don't believe this story, do you, Elsa?'

Crawley retorted. 'It's clear as the driven snow this man is a hired gunslinger. And, like as not, he's working for Steiger. All they want is to get their hands on your spread now that poor Amos is dead. We need to stick together. That's the best way to defeat these varmints.'

Elsa Durham hesitated. She was torn between the acerbic allegation of her friends and neighbours, and the charismatic persona of this mysterious newcomer.

'You can't believe the claim of some drifter who just happens by,' the protective blacksmith insisted.

The virulent accusation was ignored as Elsa held the stranger's prominent gaze. At the same time, she was desperately trying to delve beneath the hard exterior. He certainly didn't possess the rough-edged crudity redolent of Web Steiger's usual gunslicks. 'Sticking his neck out certainly didn't help my father, did it, Obe?' she declared quietly. The cutting invective was sufficient to silence any further attempt to vilify the newcomer.

Ben took advantage of this unexpected dent in the hostile mood. 'All I want is to help out, if'n you'll let me. And, according to Chico Lafferty, your pa was the man to give me the low-down. Now that he's passed on, ma'am,' he coaxed this enticing female gently, 'perhaps you would be good enough to fill me in on the trouble I seem to have accidentally stumbled into. I ain't no homesteader, so any assistance in keeping the place afloat would sure be welcome.'

Elsa considered the request, undecided as to whether she should be placing her trust in a man she barely knew. But what other option was there? The way things were shaping up in the Nueces, Web Steiger would soon be top dog, and

47

those who displayed any resistance to his evil ambitions would be wiped out, just like her father and the others who had tried to fight back. Lafferty was lucky to have escaped with his life. And it was all down to this stranger. She owed him a hearing at least.

Elsa walked over to her horse and mounted up. 'We'll ride out to my place straight away and I'll explain the situation. Then you can take a look at the books my father kept for the Jaybird.'

Before Ben could join her, Obediah Crawley stopped him. He was joined by the other mourners. 'Take advantage of that poor girl, and you'll have us to answer to, mister. She's suffered enough already and don't need more trouble from the likes of you.' More hostile muttering rippled through the gathering.

Ben stood his ground. A bleak regard panned across the surly faces. 'I may be known for hiring my gun out to the highest bidder, mister. But Chico Lafferty has placed his trust in me, and Miss Durham appears to accept that.

48

And I intend carrying out my side of the bargain.' Without waiting for a reply, he mounted up and followed the girl.

It was an hour's ride to the Durham spread. Little was said on the way out there. Both of these two unlikely associates were wondering anxiously what the future held for them. It was only when they arrived at the Durham homestead that Elsa voiced the conundrum that had been eating away at her since leaving the cemetery.

'You mentioned something about being known for your reputation,' she posed tentatively. 'Does that mean you're just another hired gun, like Rizzo?'

Needing to ensure that his response to her query hit the mark, he hesitated. The girl wrongly construed the uncertainty. 'I thought so,' she snapped. 'If'n that's the case, I want nothing more to do with you.' She turned away, displaying her disdain.

'You're right in assuming that Ben Chisum sells his gun hand for hard cash.' Elsa swung round, a look of horror warping her face. It was obvious she was cognisant of his hard-nosed repute. Seeing the abhorrent regard aimed his way, Ben anxiously hurried on, intent on clearing up the confusion. 'But unlike what you might have heard, I only step in where justice and fair play are being contested. More often than not, my guns have to do the talking. So if'n you folks want rid of Web Steiger and all he stands for, then gun law is the only thing those critters understand.'

The ardent plea for tolerance appeared to have struck the right note. Elsa's stiff manner relaxed noticeably. 'I have to admit, though,' he continued, 'hearing that Squint Rizzo had been taken on by Steiger was a huge inducement. Him and me have unfinished business.' He didn't elaborate when Elsa raised a quizzical eye. Instead, changing the subject with a warm smile, he declared, 'My mouth is drier than the desert wind. Any chance of a cup of coffee now I'm here?'

The handsome stranger's mesmerizing smile had won the girl over. It was returned with a cautious hint of coquetry as she entered the cabin.

A pot of coffee was duly brewed. Together with a plate of tasty home-made cinnamon cakes, the two rather discomfited allies sat round the table in the living room. Elsa explained in detail what was happening to their valley: how Web Steiger, as the biggest rancher with his S Bar 7 brand, had decided that he wanted the whole caboodle for raising cattle.

'We homesteaders have been treated like criminals,' Elsa averred vigorously. 'And when Pa objected, he paid the price.' Tears broke out on her face. 'Steiger has the power and money to enforce his version of the law as an excuse for removing those who refuse to up sticks and leave of their own accord. The skunk has masked his odious scheme under the banner of vigilante law, claiming all the homesteaders are stealing land reserved for cattle.'

Suddenly her grief turned to unbridled anger, mingled with frustration. A bunched fist slammed down on the table, making the cups rattle. The feeling of helplessness threatening to bubble over was writ large on every line of her face. 'And there's nobody willing or able to challenge him. My father tried; look what happened to him. Chico Lafferty would have gone down the same road if'n you hadn't stumbled on their drumhead court.'

Ben wanted desperately to reach across and comfort her, but he sensed this was not the time for such displays of affection, which might well be misconstrued. All he could offer were resolute words of support. 'With your help, I'm going to run the Jaybird until such time as this land grabber can be brought to heel.' The promises of retribution that emerged seemed trite, banal under the circumstances.

'But you're just a man alone,' Elsa protested. 'How can you go up against the S Bar 7?'

'I can try.' Blue Creek Ben Chisum had thrown his hat into the ring and there was no going back. 'That's what I do. And I have a personal angle in this now.' He held the girl's questioning regard. 'Did you witness Rizzo gun down your pa?'

The sudden outburst of emotion was quickly stifled as Elsa's lovely features dissolved into a rictus of hate. Her tiny fists bunched, the knuckles blanching. She shook her head. 'They made sure he was alone before murdering him. But I know it was Rizzo. Steiger was bragging about it when he came by later and told me the land was now up for grabs, and he wanted me out.'

'I might have known Squint Rizzo would be involved.' Ben's eyes narrowed to thin slits, promis-ing terminal reprisal. 'He and I used to be partners until the rat did the dirty on me down in Mexico. So you see, I'm in this as deep as you now.'

He was about to elucidate further when the sound of approaching horses saw both of them lurching to their feet. 'That must be Steiger now. Come to issue his final warning to quit the spread.'

A grating voice penetrated the cabin walls. 'I know you're in there, Blue Creek.

53

My boys spotted you in Maverick asking after Amos Durham. This ain't no place for you. Best you pull out while you're able. I won't be asking a second time.'

Ben was about to open the door when Elsa stayed his hand. 'Let me handle this, Ben. You go out there now and he'll gun you down for sure.'

Loath as he was to back down, the girl was already opening the door, forcing him to remain hidden. 'This is my land now, Steiger. Just 'cos you shot down my father don't change anything.'

'Amos had no signed legal claim to this land. He was shot while resisting arrest for rustling,' the gang leader snapped out, 'just like anyone else around here that bucks the rule of law. You have forty-eight hours to leave the valley.'

'Pure cold-blooded murder, that's all it was,' Elsa retorted angrily. Legs akimbo and hands on hips, she brazenly faced off this arrogant land-grabber and his bunch of lackeys. 'Your version of the law is ruled by greed and nothing else. So you can go whistle if'n you think I'm shipping out anytime soon.'

'And I'm here to back her play.' The blunt declaration came from a man standing to one side of the house. Ben had seen the way things were heading and quickly scuttled out the back door and round the side of the house to confront the unwelcome deputation from a position of strength behind a wagon. 'I'm in partnership with Chico Lafferty. We've signed a legally binding agreement for me to run the Jaybird while he's away, and there'll be more land claim registrations being made in the near future.'

Steiger laughed out loud. 'Who you trying to fool, mister? Lafferty is dead. He was put on trial and found guilty. And I have it on good authority he was hanged as a common horse thief.'

'Well, I'm telling you, mister: Lafferty is alive, if not exactly in the best of health since you left him dangling on the end of that rope. Lucky for him that I happened along, but not so lucky for you.' That unwelcome announcement was a shock that momentarily found Steiger lost for a response. 'And seeing as I now have a vested interest in the Nueces Valley, you can expect big trouble if'n any attempt is made to stop me working the land.'

Notwithstanding, Steiger quickly recovered from the stunning revelation that his plan to snatch the Jaybird had been thwarted. He leaned over the neck of his horse. 'There are five of us here and I gotten plenty more guys on the payroll. You're just one man. So any threats you make are worthless, fella.' Nonetheless, this upstart had rattled the vigilante leader. 'That reputation of your'n ain't gonna do you no good down here in south Texas. I make the law around here, and you'd do well to remember that.'

Ben was in no way overawed by the vigilante leader's threats. 'I don't see Squint Rizzo. He afraid to face me after that stunt he pulled down in Zaragoza?'

'He's carrying out more important work, exercising his particular skills to show Abe Tewksbury the best course of action for his continued good health. I'm sure the stubborn critter will reach the right decision. Squint is mighty persuasive in that direction, as I'm sure you know. He's promised to shoot you down on sight.'

'In the back if'n I'm any judge of character,' Ben scowled.

Steiger's face hardened, his back stiffening. The time for talk had run out, and this guy needed removing. 'You've had your warning, Chisum. And it looks like you're gonna ignore it. Too bad. Take him, boys!'

The four men accompanying Steiger reached for their guns immediately. Five to one were poor odds, but Ben had positioned himself well behind the wagon. His opponents were in the open, sat astride horses likely to be spooked by loud gunfire. Hot lead flew, chewing slivers of wood from the wagon sides. Ben ducked down, hustling to the back where he leaned out beside the wheel. A couple of well-placed slugs took out one of the gunmen.

As expected, the skittish mounts prevented any accurate shooting from their riders, enabling Ben to remove another man from the fracas. The victim screamed, throwing up his arms and joining his buddy in the dirt. That was enough for the remaining combatants, who threw down their guns and raised their hands.

Ben's gun hand swung to cover Web Steiger, who had backed his horse away from the line of fire. 'Looks like your boys have seen the error of their ways. How about you, Steiger?' His voice was steely hard, almost a hiss as he slipped his gun back into its holster. 'Feeling lucky, scumbag?'

Steiger's face had turned a darker shade of grey. This was not how he had expected his visit to the Durham spread to pan out. Two men down and having to eat humble pie to a hired gunslinger he would dearly love to have on his side. When he finally found his voice, it harboured a wheedling tone as he made Ben an offer. 'I could use a gun like your'n on my side. I'll pay top dollar and even give you a slice of the action. Why go up against my organization when you can be a part of making big bucks once the valley is in my hands?'

Ben hesitated as if considering the offer. 'What about Rizzo? He won't be too please having me around, seeing as it's my intention to kill the treacherous rat.'

'You leave Rizzo to me. I'll make sure he don't cause you no trouble. So, is it a deal?' Steiger leaned forward, offering a hand to clinch the agreement.

Ben's smile was icy cold, failing to reach his eyes. 'I'd rather shake hands with the Devil.' He stepped forward, six-gun palmed, and jabbed at the odious vigilante. 'I'm coming into Uvalde tomorrow to deliver my contract with Chico Lafferty to the bank for safekeeping. In Texas law that makes me a legal partner. And if'n anybody tries to stop me . . .' He left the rest of the threat unspoken, instead snapping back the Army Colt to full cock. 'Now, pick up your dead and skedaddle before I add to the total.'

Steiger growled out an epithet, gesturing for his remaining lackeys to sling the dead bodies over their mounts. 'Make no mistake, Chisum, you're gonna regret going up against me. You ain't heard the last of this, not by a long chalk. Round one may have gone your way, but there ain't no magic wand to wave down here in the Nueces. It's a week's ride to the capital in Austin, which makes me the law.' He wagged a finger, intended to add credence to his threat of intimidation. 'After what you've done today, your days are numbered, Blue Creek. And that's a pledge I mean to keep.'

Ben sniggered. 'Empty promises ain't worth a dime to me, hangman.' He stepped away from the wagon, joining the shaking figure of Elsa Durham on the cabin veranda. A comforting arm rested on her shoulder. His gun hand, however, wavered not a jot as Web Steiger and his sorry deputation departed. 'Now, sling your hook before I get really angry.'

The gang leader snarled, but he had much to think on. The hero of Blue Creek had made sure of that.

4

Dark Side of the Moon

Ben had stayed longer than intended at the Durham homestead. 'Guess I'd better be going,' he proposed somewhat regretfully, getting to his feet. In truth he was loath to leave this luscious creature, and not just because she was now alone with ruthless predators itching to get their dirty hands on her property. 'It's a long ride to the Jaybird and I want to get there before dark.'

Elsa cast a glance at the clock ticking on the wall. 'No chance of that now. It's further than you might think, and a person who has never been there could easily get lost.' Ben shuffled his feet, a heavily charged silence separating them. It was Elsa who broke the impasse. 'You could stay here and use my father's old room.' She looked away, not wishing to appear too brazen.

The tentative suggestion was initially

rejected. He figured there was still enough time to reach the Jaybird to make a cursory inspection of the holding if'n he left straight away. It was the girl's poignant observation that Steiger and his gang would likely expect that and be lying in wait to ambush him that was the clincher persuading him to accept her invitation.

In truth, it had not been a tough decision. Keeping company with this winsome girl was simplicity itself. Leaving the next morning to head for Uvalde and a confrontation with the vigilantes was going to be the hard part. She made him the best home-cooked meal he had enjoyed in a coon's age, after which business reluctantly needed to be tackled.

'Guess I better get down to examining the books your pa kept on the Jaybird,' he said, wiping the crumbs of a delicious apple pie from his lips. 'Maybe one more cup of coffee will help me concentrate.' Their eyes locked as she poured it out. Elsa quickly dragged her gaze away as the hot liquid spilled onto the table. Her embarrassment at this unfamiliar show of feeling was covered by fussing with a dishcloth. The moment passed as the two resumed their mundane chores.

It was around midnight when the horses could be heard snickering outside. Ben was about to go see what had disturbed them when Elsa appeared. Her hair was all of a tangle. And with an old shawl wrapped around her nightgown, she looked pretty as a picture. An unqualified gawp went unheeded by the innocent temptress.

'I'll go see what's disturbed them,' she said picking up a shotgun and heading for the door. 'It might be a wandering coyote hoping for easy pickings. Best you stay here, seeing as you don't know the spread like I do.'

Outside, the silver disc had just emerged from hiding. Nothing seemed to be amiss. Nevertheless, Elsa circled around, her eyes searching the shadowy recesses for any sign of unwelcome scavengers. Just when she was about to return to the cabin, a heavily calloused hand covered her mouth, effectively cutting off a scream. Her assailant's other hand snatched away the shotgun.

'Try calling out and your days on this earth are numbered,' a gruff voice scored by too much hard liquor hissed in her ear. 'Understand my drift, sister?' A fearful nod, and the hand was removed slowly.

'What are you doing here, Rizzo?' she asked, although the answer to her query was clear as the moon. 'Your old buddy is down there now if'n you want to draw him out into the open. Then again, maybe he already knows you're here and his gun is trained on you at this very moment.'

'Cut the smart cracks, lady,' Rizzo snarled, extracting the cartridges from the lethal scattergun. 'I'm holding all the aces where you're concerned. He tries any funny business and you're the one in the firing line.' And to prove his point, he held the girl in a tight grip, using her as a shield.

But Elsa Durham was no meek-and-mild wall-flower. Her initial terror at being waylaid soon dissipated, enabling her to play on the fear of all bushwhackers. 'Guess you didn't expect to encounter any opposition sneaking up after dark,' she rasped in his ear. 'Too bad the horses spooked your cheap stunt.'

'It don't matter none,' Rizzo growled, squeezing off the retort. 'There'll be other times to finish him off.' Then he raised his voice, sufficient for Ben to hear. 'Mistress Luck and your lady friend here have saved your bacon this time, old buddy. But I'll be waiting in Uvalde tomorrow. Don't disappoint me by playing chicken. You hear me, Blue Creek?'

Only the sighing of the night wind in a clump of cottonwoods disturbed the silence. The moon chose that moment to sidle back into the comforting seclusion of a bank of cloud, allowing Rizzo to disappear behind the barn where his horse was tied. Elsa returned to the cabin to be met on the veranda by her houseguest. 'I heard him,' Ben averred. 'And before you try dissuading me, I have every intention of going in there tomorrow and lodging that agreement with the bank.'

'But you heard what he said, Ben,' the girl pleaded, gripping his arms. 'The skunk will be waiting to gun you down. If'n they return with more men, we could always hide in the secret tunnel Pa built to escape from Indian raiders.' She lifted a rug to reveal the hidden trapdoor.

'I don't think so,' was the measured and somewhat choked reply. This girl really appeared to be concerned for his safety. 'I need to do this my way. No skulking like a rat in a hole.' At that moment they were very close. He could have kissed her and knew in his heart she would have responded. And he almost did. But there was too much at stake. Allowing unfettered emotions to blur his resolve would only bring complications he could well do without, so he gently eased her away.

Yet, deep down, both of them knew that a line had been crossed. Never before had the tough Ben Chisum allowed a woman to pluck at his heartstrings.

Elsa Durham had unwittingly strayed into that private domain and upset the apple cart. The unsettling moment was brusquely pushed aside with some reluctance.

'Steiger won't try any gunplay on the streets of Uvalde,' he said, reasserting a more businesslike manner. 'Even he wouldn't be stupid enough to think he could get away with cold-blooded murder in front of all those witnesses. He needs to maintain the illusion, however feeble, that he's upholding the law.' A slack smile went some way to appeasing his reserved stance. 'Now, let's get some shuteye. I, for one, need a clear head for what needs to be done tomorrow.'

But sleep evaded him. Ben couldn't settle knowing he would soon be entering the lion's den. He would need all his courage and nerves of steel to face down Web Steiger and his crew. Not to mention the treacherous Squint Rizzo. Yet, somehow, tiredness managed to claim him and he finally nodded off, helped by tremulous visions of a flaxon-haired angel.

The next thing he knew, a rooster was

vigorously announcing the arrival of the new day. An early morning sun beamed in through the window. In any other circumstances it would have heralded an idyllic future. His thoughts focused on movement in the other room.

Elsa was already outside. Daisy the cow still needed milking and the hens needed feeding. She made sure the inner man was satisfied, at least, by cooking him a hearty breakfast. Newly laid eggs and home-cured bacon made him fully cognisant of where his future lay. No two-bit land-grabber was going to force this delectable woman from her land.

Further attempts to warn him off making any rash decisions fell accordingly on deaf ears. Ben Chisum was now more determined than ever to carry out his mission, come hell or high water. A peck on the cheek as he was mounting up almost changed his mind, reminding him of the acute peril he would soon be facing. The hesitant musing immediately caught the attention of Old Nick himself. A fawning voice, laced with sycophantic flattery, whispered silently in his ear.

Why risk everything on the whim of fate when you could so easily ride away in the company of this pretty girl? Only heartache and death lie at the end of the road to Uvalde. *He quickly shrugged off the tempter's weaselling inducements. That was not the Blue Creek way.*

A curled lip spoke of the need for justice and right. And then there was his promise to Chico Lafferty, not to mention that unfinished business with Squint Rizzo. He had to see this through to the bitter end, no matter how it turned out. He would never be able to live with himself otherwise. The beguiling lure of the horned demon had challenged him before and he had come away unscathed. And so it would be this time as well. The words of the Good Book immediately came to mind: *Get thee behind me, Satan!*

He threw a kiss to the girl of his dreams and rode away, heading into unknown waters without looking back. Had he done so, Elsa Durham's beseeching regard might well have been too much even for the stoically resourceful Blue Creek Ben Chisum to resist.

5

Unexpected Box of Tricks

Uvalde was a busy township; a focus for commerce in the Nueces Valley, and Web Steiger wanted to be in control. He already owned various premises in the town, including the Burning Bush saloon, outside which he was standing. A half-dozen of his men ranged idly on either side. All eyes were turned towards the southern end of town, the direction from which Ben Chisum was expected.

Squint Rizzo drew his pistol and checked the load. He spun the trigger guard on his middle finger expertly, before dropping the gun back into its holster. It was a flamboyant piece of showmanship intended to impress.

Steiger merely scowled. 'Fancy stage-acting like that don't impress me,' he rapped out. 'You had your chance last night and you blew it. There'll be no gunplay in Uvalde unless Chisum starts it,' was the boss's curt order.

'Why not get it over with fast?' Rizzo retorted. 'I can take him easy.'

'While you're on my payroll, mister, you'll obey orders like everyone else.'

Steiger leaned in close. 'Start a gun battle here and the authorities will be down on our necks lickety split. Any killing that needs carrying out has to be on the sly or in self-defence. Got that, Squint?'

Surreptitious glances from passing citizens were aimed at the vigilante gathering. Fear mingled uneasily with doubt. That was what self-styled law under the diktat of a vigilance committee meant. Steiger knew that he needed a semblance of legitimacy for the town to support him and give him the power base to further his dubious ends.

Ruthless actions could easily be squared away where no witnesses could object. Here, he needed to act under the banner of vigilante law aimed at bringing order to a territory where no official control existed. Blasting a guy like Blue

Creek Chisum out of the saddle would require too much explaining away.

Rizzo shrugged. 'It's your call . . . boss. So, how do you plan to stop him delivering that agreement? Just walk up and ask him nicely?'

The sneering jibe was ignored as Steiger crossed the street to intercept the man who would do just that, but in his own inimitable manner. 'Howdy there, Gus,' he greeted an ox of a man who had just stepped out of the hardware store where he worked. 'You still want the piece of Jaybird land I promised if'n you'd do me that little favour we talked about earlier?'

The lumbering simpleton paused, his sluggish brain trying to recall what had been discussed. Steiger concealed his impatience. 'Remember? I asked you to prevent Blue Creek Chisum from depositing a document at the bank in the way you know best.' He held up his fists, tiny in comparison, being dwarfed by the huge plates dangling beside the hulking gorilla.

Gus Ordway hesitated. 'I d-don't know, Mister Steiger. K-killing a man ain't to be taken l-lightly', he stuttered out slowly.

'I seem to recall you dishing out some brutal treatment against Cash Arbuckle; ended badly for him.'

'That was different,' Ordway protested. 'He'd been making my life hell. Calling me the town gump all the danged time. I couldn't take no more.' Gus was quite content to be called Bucktooth Ordway. That was how he'd been born. But when local tearaways began labelling him 'the Gump', it made him see red. Cash Arbuckle had paid the ultimate price for his sleazy attempt to humiliate him.

'Killing is killing, Gus. I've kept it quiet so far. But if'n the authorities found out, you'd be heading for the final countdown for sure. This way it stays our secret and you get that land you've always hankered after. We can always say he started it.'

'Guess you're right there,' the ox nodded. 'OK, then, I'll do it.'

'You just need to make sure he throws

the first punch, then it'll be self-defence.'
Steiger breathed a sigh of relief. And just
in time as well. Laredo had signalled that
their quarry had been spotted entering
the southern end of town. 'So, you know
what to do?' he pressed Ordway.

The hulk nodded, flexing his ham-like
paws as he stepped out into the middle
of the street. It was against his simple
code of ethics to fight somebody without a good reason. But the vigilante boss
was threatening to reveal his fatal error
of judgement. What choice did he have?
None, it seemed.

Steiger returned to the Burning Bush
and a ringside seat to watch the show.
Ben swung into the main street to be met
by a man mountain barring his way. He
nudged his horse to avoid the obstruction. Ordway followed, forcing him to
pull up.

'I can't allow you to reach the bank,
mister,' the man declared somewhat
reluctantly. He was loath to start a ruckus
with someone whom he had nothing
against. But Steiger had him over a

barrel. And that promise of land for a guy like him was the icing on the cake: the chance to walk tall instead of being regarded as the town imbecile. 'Best you turn round and ride away.'

'I can't do that, fella,' Ben replied, nudging his horse forward and barging Ordway aside. But the hulk was not so easily dislodged. He grabbed hold of the reins and made to pull Ben out of the saddle. A boot slammed into the hulk's chest, throwing him off balance. He fell into the dust.

Ben took the opportunity to dismount and remove his gun-belt, slinging it over the saddle horn. And there he waited in the middle of the street, watching as his aggressor struggled to his feet. Ordway was momentarily unsure what had occurred; it was normally him who dished out the hard knocks. The abashed look he aimed at this confident stranger was wrapped in a steely determination to turn the tables on the embarrassing prelude. 'You shouldn't have done that, mister. Now I'm gonna have to beat your brains out.'

Ben hunkered down into the classic prizefighter's stance. One of his early jobs in Roswell, New Mexico had been as bodyguard to the territory's leading exponent of the noble art of boxing, a newly-arrived contact sport brought over the big ocean from Europe. Bare-knuckle fighting was giving ground to this far more sophisticated sport where skill was considered much more valid than explicit brutality. How a fighter moved about the ring, his defence as well as attack, was encouraged under the auspices of rules devised by the Marquis of Queensbury.

Gentleman Johnny Monkton was an acknowledged exponent of the craft. It also attracted unscrupulous villains who saw their dubious livelihoods dis-appearing. As a result, Monkton needed protection and Blue Creek Chisum made the perfect minder. Unfortunately, prior to the sport becoming popularized the prize money was small. An agreement was reached accordingly, by which Ben was instructed in the main principles as part-payment for his services.

The ungainly stance of the fighters initially caused much guffawing and sniping until it was realized that skilled proponents of Queensbury's system were outsmarting their opponents. Guile and slick footwork were enabling them to win far more contests against traditional brawlers.

Gus Ordway was one of those who figured brute force would solve all his problems. It had worked so far. But Gus did not know his own strength, a mistake that led to his current obligation to Web Steiger, who had secretly witnessed the lethal fracas with Cash Arbuckle.

He stared open-mouthed at the clownish antics of his adversary, a lean-limbed fella jumping about like a marionette. Gus hawked out a brittle guffaw. 'What sort of fancy fighting is this?' was the derisory comment as he settled down into his customary gorilla-like posture. 'You figuring to beat me by dancing around?'

Ordway didn't wait for a reply to his caustic jibe. Hoping to catch this jack-a-dandy flat-footed, he rushed in, arms swinging haymaker style. Had they landed, the fight would have been over before it even got started. But Ben was ready for him. He ducked aside quickly as the swingeing tree trunks whistled by overhead.

Thrown off balance, Ordway rumbled by receiving a stiff one-two in his midriff. The punches were well aimed, forcing the hulk to his knees, clutching at his stomach. A second solid left pummelled his exposed jaw. A gasp went up from the watching audience as blood dribbled from a cut lip. They had seen Gus in action before, but never on the receiving end.

Ben stepped back, gesturing for his opponent to get up. Ordway's brain was quickly arriving at the painful conclusion that this guy was no tenderfoot. He lumbered to his feet. But Gumpy Gus did not have the aptitude to alter his style of fighting, and for a man of his bulk he could move surprisingly fast when the situation demanded.

He stepped forward, catching Ben high on the head with a hard fist that rattled his teeth. Luckily, he was able to duck underneath the follow-up, sidestepping out of range before the ox could grab him in a deadly bear hug. Ben shook the pulp from his brain as Ordway sensed the tide was turning in his favour.

Unfortunately, the lucky strike had made him less cautious. He made to grab the pugilist, but his lumbering gait played into the hands of his nimble-footed adversary, who easily evaded the clumsy manoeuvring.

Ben's dodging around only served to incense the Gump, who had no answer to such alien tactics. 'Stand still and fight proper,' he shouted in exasperation. But the plea went unheeded as yet another straight left hammered the exposed chin. Ben followed it up with a right hook that connected with a solid thwack to Ordway's head. The slow-witted brawler staggered back, struggling to fend off the flurry of bruising, well-placed punches that came his way.

But he was not beaten yet. A stubborn will not to surrender drove the big guy forward. Grabbing a heavy sack of pinto beans as if it were a feather pillow, he hurled it at the object of his humiliation. Ben stepped aside, the whole caboodle splitting open and scattering the contents every which way. This failure to crush his opponent appeared to dishearten the man, his long ungainly arms falling to his side.

Ben surmised this could be a ruse inducing him to lower his guard. Fights of this nature were never over until the winner decreed otherwise. And this jigger was still on his feet. Nimbly leaning in, he delivered a couple of punishing blows to the body, following up with a brutal uppercut. Ordway tipped over, crashing into a stack of barrels, which sent him flying.

Still not ready to surrender, he lumbered to his feet, hoping for one final chance to turn the tables. But it was not to be. Easily blocking the ungainly swipes, Ben delivered the *coup de grace*, splaying his doughty opponent across a nearby hitching rail. And there Gus Ordway hung like a discarded saddle blanket, blood dribbling from a myriad cuts. He had finally met his match.

Not wishing to dish out any undue punishment once his challenger had been defeated, Ben stepped back, wiping the sweat from his brow and breathing deep. It was a long time since he had needed to exercise his boxing skills, and this guy had put up a good show. But saloon brawling was never going to prevail over a skilled tactician except if sheer bad luck took a hand in the proceedings.

The bizarre contest had lasted for a little over two minutes. He rubbed his scraped knuckles, staring at the static hulk and wondering why this guy had challenged him. The answer was forthcoming as a leering Squint Rizzo stepped down into the street.

Steiger had seen the way the contrived

situation was leaning, and it was not going in his favour. The Gump was living up to his repugnant name. The clumsy knucklehead's lethal mitts were of no use against this new type of fighting. He had witnessed a similar contest the previous year in Austin. Something had to be done to regain the ascendancy.

'You can take him now, Squint,' he ordered the gunman. 'Fancy footwork ain't got no chance against hot lead. If'n anybody takes offence, we can say that Chisum was going to finish the Gump off and you stepped in to defend him. I'll deal with that useless hulk later.'

Rizzo's face broke into an ugly grimace as his hand dropped to the butt of the Army Remington. Here was his chance to remove a thorn in his flesh. 'Didn't I tell you this is the only way?' he mouthed, stepping off the boardwalk.

All of Ben's attention was focused on the defeated giant as he drew breath into his heaving lungs. He just stood there, oblivious to the deadly threat posed by his nemesis. Before Rizzo could draw his pistol, however, a cutting voice stayed his hand.

6

Curly Bill Takes a Hand

'Pull that stunt and your guts will be splattered all over the street.' A hefty jasper boasting a large, drooping moustache stepped out from the shelter of an alley. An unlit cigar poked from between gritted teeth. All eyes swung towards the origin of the brittle warning. 'The rest of you rannies, toss your hardware into the street.'

Ben's startled expression matched those of his adversaries. He was no less surprised to see this visitor from his past. But it was the sawn-off shotgun pointing at Rizzo that caught everyone's attention. It was a deadly spur not to be challenged.

Yet only Buckshot Roberts moved to obey. A finger traced a rough course across his disfigurement. The sight of those twin barrels had made his blood run cold. The others stood their ground, unsure of themselves, and waited on the boss's reaction to this unexpected intervention.

The newcomer sensed a hint of refusal, a weighing up of the odds. He quickly stymied any imprudent retaliation. 'That means now, boys, else my friend here does the talking.' He wagged the shotgun. Half-a-dozen shooters immediately bit the dust. The shotgun wielder's stiff posture relaxed. 'That sure was some fancy footwork, old buddy,' he said without taking his hawkish gaze off the vigilantes. 'Guess we got some catching up to do since the old days.'

Ben smiled. The same old, humorous twinkle mixed with a sly half smirk testified to this guy not being easily alarmed. No change there then. Ben hadn't seen his old sidekick in eight years.

'Curly Bill Redleg!' Ben ejaculated in shocked surprise. 'That shooter you're toting sure don't get any smaller, do it? And I see you're still wearing them boot trimmings.'

'Makes life more interesting,' was the

brisk rejoinder. 'Where in blue blazes did you learn to fight like that?'

'It's a long story, old buddy. I'll tell you later. More to the point, what are you doing in Uvalde?'

The two old friends had met up during the war when they ran with a ruthless band of guerrilla raiders, known as Jennison's Jayhawkers, who operated in Kansas. The red sheepskin topping on the left boot was primarily for identification. But it soon came to symbolize the ruthless style of undercover warfare waged by the group.

Such was their notorious reputation that the Northern authorities ordered those caught to be shot on sight. Ben and his pard managed to evade capture and instead became expert snipers for the Southern cause under General Robert E. Lee. After the signing of the peace in 1865, the pair split up and went their separate ways.

'Came looking for you, Blue Creek,' was the studied reply. 'Your name came up in conversation while I was taking a well-earned rest in Amarillo. Rumour had it you were having a spot of bother with the *federales* down Mexico way. Figured you might need some help. Seems I was mistaken.'

'No mistake, pal. I got out of that hell hole by the skin of my teeth.' Ben's icy gaze shifted to the stunned face of Squint Rizzo. 'No thanks to some low-down Judas who sold me down the river. Keep that scattergun nice and steady, Bill. Reckon it's time to even the score.' He walked over to his horse and fastened on the gun-belt, settling the rig into its customary position.

'You do what you have to, Creek. I'll keep these gents company while we watch some more fancy action. That sure was some performance you gave this here gorilla.' Gus Ordway groaned, struggling to comprehend what had happened.

Slowly, but with deliberation, Ben walked across and stood no more than two feet from his old partner. 'Pick up your gun, Squint. We can finish this here and now. Just you and me. None of these guys will interfere. Can't say fairer than that.'

'You take me for a fool, Chisum?' Rizzo snarled back. 'I kill you, and Redleg would gun me down straight away.' Rizzo had ridden with the infamous Clarke Quantrille. Though fighting for the Confederate cause, neither faction had ever met up to discuss tactics. Nevertheless, the individual names and reps of Jennison's Jayhawkers were well known. 'We can finish this some other time when your pal ain't around to protect you.'

Ben gave the wheedling riposte a mocking snort of disdain. 'In that case, you can have this to be going on with.' A bunched fist, still skinned from its recent encounter with Gus Ordway, shot out and connected with Rizzo's chin. It packed all the energy and power its owner could muster. Rizzo's head snapped back, his wobbly legs giving way as he tumbled into the dust.

'Goldarn it, Creek, for a skinny dude, you sure pack a mean punch,' the impressed Redleg enthused.

The compliment was acknowledged with a curt nod before he snapped at the bemused turncoat. 'Like you said, jerk, we'll meet up again. But next time, I won't be so lenient.' He then turned his attention to Web Steiger. 'I'm going over to the bank now to register my claim, which allows me to run the Jaybird until such time as Chico Lafferty chooses to return from his enforced vacation. Anybody tries to stop me and Curly Bill here has my permission to ventilate their hide.'

The double-barrelled scattergun ensured that no resistance was forthcoming from the cowed vigilantes. Having recovered his senses, Gus Ordway crawled away beneath the boardwalk. Such was his feeling of humiliation he would dearly have loved for the ground to swallow him up, but it was too hard. So he contented himself with disappearing before Steiger made good his threat of retribution.

Nobody knew nor cared now about Ordway's whereabouts. All Web Steiger could do was watch powerlessly while that vital delivery was made to the bank. His men were equally ineffective, shuffling their feet and confined to throwing toothless scowls at the grinning gun-toter.

Five minutes later, Ben returned. 'So, where to now?' Curly Bill enquired. 'My arm's getting mighty tired holding this hogleg steady.'

'Somewhere we can rest up and make plans.'

'Now that's a place I ain't never been before. Lead on, pal.'

Before they mounted up, Ben had strong words for the leader of the vigilantes. 'As of now, Jaybird land is off limits, you turkeys. Anybody crosses the divide and I'll be within my rights to stop them. You've been warned.'

'You won't get away with this, Chisum,' Steiger retorted. 'There are too many of us for you to hold that section alone.'

'I ain't alone anymore.' He turned to Curly Bill. 'You with me, buddy?'

'Need you ask?'

The two old sidekicks backed away, retrieving their horses gingerly and mounting up. That was the moment Steiger made his move. Circumspection was thrown to the wind. 'Get 'em, boys', he called out. 'Don't let the skunks leave town.' The vigilantes were about to reach for their discarded weapons when the booming shotgun dug a hole in the street, scattering the hardware in all directions.

Forced back, the breathing space supplied by Redleg's deadly shooter enabled the fugitives to hightail it out of Uvalde, leaving Web Steiger once again fuming helplessly. But not for long. 'Why are you turkeys standing around here like fairground dummies?' he railed angrily. 'Get your horses and go after those skunks, pronto. There's a fifty dollar bonus on each of their heads — dead or alive!'

'Where they headed, boss?' Laredo asked foolishly.

The writhing serpent on Steiger's livid purple face threatened to strike. He was in no mood for such ludicrous questions. 'Where in hell's name do you think, bonehead? The Jaybird homestead, of course. Didn't you hear that dude say he was gonna run the place while Lafferty skulks away in some hole? Well, that ain't gonna happen. Now shift your asses and get after them.'

That pecuniary incentive certainly spurred the men into action. The only problem was the horses had been left down by the livery stable at the opposite end of town. Valuable time was lost while the gang retrieved them, giving Chisum and his buddy plenty of time to skedaddle.

'You stay here, Squint,' he said to the hired gunman. 'I need you to find Ordway and make sure he disappears . . . permanently.'

'Be my pleasure, boss. Maybe that's worth a bonus as well?'

Steiger snorted. 'Don't push your luck, mister. Just get the job done before we discuss any bonus. So far, Chisum has easily outwitted you. I ain't paying out good dough for failure.' Without uttering another word, he stumped back into the saloon. After a morning like this he badly needed a drink.

Meanwhile, the two fugitives were

making good their escape. On leaving the northern limits of Uvalde, Gus Ordway appeared suddenly from behind a grain store. Ben immediately palmed his pistol and aimed it at the burly hulk. The notion that he was intent on completing the task assigned by Steiger was at the forefront of his thinking. A bruised and blooded countenance did nothing to allay his suspicions.

Ordway was astute enough to have grasped that his sudden manifestation might give a false impression of his motives. A conciliatory hand was raised as he drew level. 'Hold your fire, mister. I ain't got nothing against you. Fact is, I'd like to join up with you.'

Ben's brow puckered in a frown of puzzlement. 'Just keep your distance, fella, and say your piece. One false move and you're dog meat.'

Observing the hesitation etched across Chisum's face, the giant pressed home his request. 'I want nothing more to do with Steiger and the kind of law he's after pushing in the Nueces. I might not be too well endowed up here.' He tapped his large skull. 'But I can still shoot straight and I know the valley better'n most.' A smile broke across the big man's bruised features. 'And I would sure appreciate you teaching me that new way of fighting.'

Ben was still undecided. Nevertheless, he could see that this guy was incapable of effecting any meaningful degree of duplicity. 'What do you reckon, Curly? Do we need a guy that just tried to beat my brains to a pulp?' He winked at his pal.

Redlegs thought for a moment before answering.

'I figure if'n one of them punches had landed it would have considerably improved your ugly kisser no end,' was the equally droll rejoinder. Ordway just looked on vacantly. The lively banter was beyond the comprehension of the slow-witted booby. 'Maybe a dancing lesson will help with the revamp.'

'I know this country better than anybody around here,' Ordway insisted, thinking they were going to refuse his request. 'And I sure ain't afraid of hard work if'n you need someone to help run the Jaybird.'

'A fella that likes work scores heavily in my book, buddy,' Redleg interjected, still refusing to take life seriously. 'He can do my share anytime.'

'Guess my pard here is all for you joining us,' Ben concurred, maintaining a straight face. 'And I always value his opinion — if not his sad view of my good looks. Glad to have you on my side, Gus.' He held out a hand.

Now that kind of gesture was something the big fella did understand. He grabbed the proffered mitt, forcing a painful wince out of Ben as the big man's enthusiastic reaction almost crushed it. 'Gee, much obliged, Mister Chisum,' he gushed. 'You won't regret it.'

Removing the throbbing member gently, Ben shook some life back into it. 'I sure hope so. Another gun is always welcome, not to mention a helping hand if'n mine ever manages to recover.'

For the first time, a beaming smile broke across the giant's rubbery face. 'Sorry about that, boss. I sometime don't know my own strength.' There was no disagreement there, nor any resentment. Ben was glad to have the burly brawler on his side. Gus Ordway might not have all his marbles in one bag, but he appeared to know the country like the back of his hand. Neither he nor Curly Bill had that vital knowledge at their fingertips.

7

Shortening the Odds

The three *amigos* rode side-by-side at a steady canter. While his two companions discussed future tactics, Ordway remained silent, a permanent grin etched across his scabrous features. The guileless simpleton was content to bask in the envious position of having been accepted into the ranks of such notable company.

Ben kept turning around repeatedly to check if they were being followed. He was certain that Steiger would not sit idly by and allow the loss of face suffered in Uvalde to go unavenged. Their destination was Jaybird land, and that was where Gus Ordway's knowledge of the terrain would become paramount.

They had been riding for half an hour when Ben spotted a rising column of dust some two miles behind them.

'Looks like we ain't alone,' he

remarked, spurring the chestnut to the gallop. The others kept pace. The puerile smile slipped from Ordway's face as the realization dawned that he had likely stepped from the frying pan into the fire. He quickly shook off the fearful notion. Anything was better than having to suffer the taunts and humiliation heaped on him previously. For once in his life, Gus Ordway, no longer a witless gump, could hold his head high.

'And judging by that dust cloud,' Ben carried on, 'there's at least eight of them on our tail. How far to the homestead, Gus?' he asked.

'We still have another hour's ride, boss,' was the rueful response.

Ben gritted his teeth, knowing there was every chance those jaspers could shorten the distance and catch up before they arrived. Somehow they had to be waylaid. Then an idea popped into his head. 'Remember that stunt we pulled at Horse Creek outside Carthage?' he said, addressing his old buddy.

'You mean when that bluecoat column

was after us and we sneakily captured their back markers?'

Ben gave a ready nod. His next question was for Ordway. It was a shouted request, competing with the wind tugging at their hats as they careered onward. 'Is there a narrow ravine close by we could lead these critters through? It has to be a somewhere that forces them down to walking pace and in single file.'

The giant didn't need to think it out. He spat out the perfect location in the next breath. A finger pointed forward. 'Sidewinder Gulch is around two miles ahead,' he asserted, eager to play his part. 'Sounds like just the place you're looking for. The trail is no more than five feet wide, with boulders rising to steep cliffs, hemming it in. And it twists and turns for another mile before breaking out onto the plains beyond. Does that sound right for what you have in mind?'

Ben leaned across and slapped the big guy on the back. 'Reckon it was my lucky day coming up against you, Gus.'

Ordway's lumpen features cracked in

a grin wider than the Rio Grande as he rubbed his aching jaw. 'I'm hoping the same can be said for me, boss.' He then added, 'But we'll need to leave a clear trail for them to follow because it's off the usual route to the Jaybird.'

Soon after, Ordway indicated the direction to take. Leaving the well-used trail, they crossed a shallow wash, making sure to leave clear sets of hoof prints their pursuers couldn't fail to spot. They were now entering broken country dominated by mesquite and fallen rocks, a desolate landscape that became increasing rough to traverse, forcing the riders down to a walk. Rounding a rocky promontory, the cutting of Sidewinder Gulch could be seen ahead: a deep gash in the wall of rock seemingly chopped by some mighty axe. Darkly forbidding, it was the only way forward.

Once inside the confines of the gulch, Ben signalled a halt. The horses were tethered behind a large clump of rocks. He extracted his lariat and gestured for Curly Bill to do likewise. 'You know what to do, buddy?' He didn't need to ask.

'We take the last two riders off'n their horses, and Gus here clubs them down before any warning cry can be given.' Both men looked at the big guy. 'This is where them big mitts of your'n come in handy,' Redleg stressed.

'Remember, Gus,' Ben added firmly, 'not a sound. The first the others must know about the ambush is when they emerge from the ravine. They won't know what's happened and will double back to search for their pals.'

'And that's when they'll get the shock of their lives,' added Redleg.

'OK, boys, let's get in position. They'll be along pronto.' Ben and Redleg secreted themselves behind a clump of chollah cactus on one side of the trail, holding their lariats ready, with Ordway crouched behind a boulder opposite. The dead branch clutched in his huge fist looked like a twig.

Within minutes, the steady clip of hoofs assailed their ears. One by one the riders passed, completely unaware of the trap into which they had been lured. All eyes were facing forward. Once the sixth man had passed, the twirling loops snaked out, encircling both necks of the last two riders simultaneously.

A quick yank to tighten the nooses and the two men were dragged off their horses. The unfortunate pair had been lagging behind the rest due to one of their horses having developed a limp. The guy called Creedy had stopped further back to dig a stone out of the horse's hoof. His buddy, Swede Larson, had waited to keep him company. They had only caught up with the others just as they were about to enter the gulch.

Even before they had hit the ground, Ordway dashed out from hiding. A swift bludgeoning effectively removed any chance of a warning shout from Larsen, who had recovered first. There was no problem with Creedy, knocked out cold by a stray hoof. The whole operation had been completed in little over ten seconds. The rest of the gang were already disappearing round the next bend, completely oblivious to the sudden removal of their sidekicks.

Ben patted both his partners on the back. 'A classic Jayhawker trick,' he whispered. 'Now we string the bastards up to that tree by their heels, but not before we strip them down to their one-piece.' Hearty chuckles greeted this final exhibition of degrading theatre. 'And now we wait to make certain our ploy works.'

Ordway's face dropped. 'What happens if'n they carry on?'

'Don't worry, Gus,' Curly gently chided. 'Likelihood is they'll abandon the pursuit and return to Uvalde. The shock of seeing those dirty pink bodies swaying in the breeze will be enough to knock the fight out of them.'

'And just to make sure they get the message,' Ben butted in, 'we'll stay here and watch what happens. If'n they do decide to carry on to the Jaybird, we'll have to persuade them it ain't a healthy choice.' He tapped his rifle.

They didn't have to wait long. Ten minutes later, the reduced line of riders gingerly appeared around the far bend. Looking far less confident than when they had entered the Sidewinder, wary eyes flicked around, fearful of what they might encounter. It was Bug Pincher who spotted the swaying pink bodies ahead. Guns drawn, the riders paused, staring wide-eyed and apprehensive before approaching the macabre sight gingerly. To dismayed peepers, the bent figures swinging gently back and forth gave the appearance of two haunches of raw meat.

The hidden watchers couldn't help but chuckle quietly at the alarm gripping the anxious vigilantes. They could hear the panic-stricken voices easily, expressed by men ignorant and fearful of what had befallen them. It was the pragmatic Buckshot Roberts who provided the answer. 'It's obvious, ain't it? Those crafty varmints have hoodwinked us into following this trail, then ambushed the two back markers.'

'That's Creedy and Larson,' enunciated a buckskin-clad former trapper called Foxy Janus. 'They were the last two because of that limping cayuse.'

'Forget about them clowns,' Roberts declared. 'The critters that did it could still be around.' Nervous eyes scanned the surrounding rocks.

To avert the panic threatening to overwhelm his men, Laredo, who was in charge of the supposed hunters — now the hunted — issued a curt order. 'Cut them down, Bug. The rest of you, keep your eyes peeled and your guns handy. Like Buckshot so rightly observed, they could be watching our every move.' The tremulous voice quivered with nervous trepidation as he and his men followed.

Pincher gingerly made his way across to the hanging tree. His feet felt like lead. Sweat bubbled up on his forehead. Breath emerged from an open maw in quick pants as he approached the supine bodies feeling totally exposed like a sitting duck. Gulping back his fear, Bug hacked at the ropes holding his sidekicks.

The inert bodies were heaved onto the abandoned horses and led cautiously back down the narrow ravine. Nothing moved to hint at the presence of the exhilarated spectators. Beyond the confines of Sidewinder Gulch, heavy breathing slowly returned to normal as the gang allowed their tension to disperse. Feeble jokes were aimed at the two underdressed suckers, but they lacked any mirth; hollow attempts to staunch the fear that gripped their innards. Each man knew it could easily have been any one of them caught out.

'What we gonna do now, Laredo?' asked a lanky jigger called Stringbean. 'Push on and those jaspers could be just waiting to mount another ambush further ahead.' This notion generated a muttering of agreement. None of the men were anxious to continue the hunt following their unsettling calamity. It was fortunate that apart from pride, nobody had been hurt.

A thoroughly niggled Laredo ignored the query. Pouring a canteen of water over the two victims, he then kicked them to instil life back into their aching bodies. 'On your feet, you two.'

The two victims stirred but were unable to appreciate what had occurred. Larson groaned, 'What happened? My head fells like it's been kicked by a mule.' His pal gingerly rubbed his scalp. A startled yelp was emitted when his hand came away coated in blood.

'We've been suckered,' rasped Buckshot, putting them both straight about what had occurred. A couple of the more sympathetic vigilantes lent Larson and Creedy their slickers. At least the yellow coverings offered some dignity to shattered self-esteem.

Without uttering another word, Laredo mounted up, heading back the way they had come. He spurred to the gallop, anxious to distance himself from Sidewinder Gulch. The others were no less eager to accompany him back to Uvalde. All the bluster allied to the chase had been crushed. This guy Chisum was certainly living up to his reputation. Web Steiger had gotten a tough fight on his hands.

★ ★ ★

Steiger knew something was wrong when they entered the Burning Bush. 'What are you guys doing back here so soon?' he snapped out, glazed eyes pinning Laredo to the spot. The cowed hardcase swallowed tentatively, apprising the vigilante leader of the crushing debacle. A bubbling rage gripped Steiger, turning his face a livid hue of purple. 'Why didn't you bunch of milksops try flushing them out?'

The scathing rebuke was received in silence. Nobody wanted to remove the focus of the boss's ire from Laredo. 'I send eight men to hunt down two,' he began, unaware that Gus Ordway had joined the rebels, 'and they make monkeys out of the lot of you, and without firing a shot.' He snatched up a glass of whisky and downed it in a single gulp. 'What in tarnation am I paying you for?'

In truth, he knew the gang had been outwitted through no fault of its own. It was anger at having been duped that was boiling over. He paced up and down the room, his mind churning. No way was this interfering gunslinger going to thwart his plans for a complete takeover in the Nueces. He had enough men, and could easily hire in more if'n the need arose.

Eventually Steiger's anger simmered down and the scheming strategist was able to think straight. He moved across to the bar. A drink of Scotch whisky would help him figure out a fresh strategy. 'A bottle of the best,' he rapped at the bartender. Shifty Ferret immediately left the other customers to serve the boss, who was noted for his virulent temper if kept waiting.

Grabbing the neck of the bottle, he downed a hefty slug. A scornful gaze rested on the back of Squint Rizzo. The gunman was avidly regaling his cronies with tales of derring-do, from which he inevitably emerged the winner. Steiger now saw the cocky braggart for a mere amateur compared to Ben Chisum.

And judging by Chisum's actions

during his brief spell in the Nueces, those stories about his town-taming exploits were clearly no figment of a lurid imagination. So far, he had easily outwitted Steiger and his superior force. And Curly Bill Redleg was not far behind. Together, they were a formidable opposition to his plans. His mouth twisted in disdain. If only he had those two on his payroll, his ambition to be top dog in the valley would be assured.

Another scowl and a second gulp of whisky merely confirmed the inadequacy of the current situation. Clearly, a fresh approach was needed. Head bowed, he stared into the mirror behind the bar. The face that gawped back at him looked drawn and haggard. Was this the Web Steiger who had struck fear into the local populace with his ruthless brand of vigilante law?

He growled out loud, causing heads to turn. 'Now that we've allowed that skunk to take over the Jaybird, at least we know his whereabouts,' he mumbled under his breath, mulling over the best way to thwart the wily coyote. 'But there's still only two of them.' A hand strayed to the livid scar carving a wayward path across the scowling countenance.

Once again, he peered at the reflection in the mirror. His eyes now glittered wildly. A new resolve had replaced the beaten man of moments before. Fingers snapped, a sure fire sign of the boss having arrived at a plan of action. His next, much more upbeat declaration found the gang emitting a collective sigh of relief as they gathered round.

'Chisum is gonna need supplies, which means leaving the homestead. They sure won't come here,' he averred eagerly. 'And Maverick is two days' ride. That's when we'll strike hard and fast. After your ham-fisted performance in Sidewinder Gulch, they won't be expecting a fast response. This is our chance to burn the place down while they're away. And when they return, we'll be waiting to give them another hot reception.' He chuckled uproariously as the resulting image of his scorching plan impinged itself on his scheming brain.

It was Rizzo who pointed out the fly in the ointment. 'Even with Chisum pushing up the daisies, you still can't take ownership of the land while Chico Lafferty is still alive.'

The objection was given short shrift. 'Once Chisum has gone to meet the Grim Reaper, you'll have plenty of time to flush that critter out of his hidey hole. And for your sake, it had better be more successful than your search for the Gump.'

Rizzo gritted his teeth, forcing back the cutting reposte regarding Steiger's own failure to finish the half-breed off with a rope. The hired gunman was rapidly coming to the conclusion that he could do a much better job of spreading the vigilante message. For the present, however, he would bide his time and swallow down any critical remarks.

Steiger then called across to Stringbean. 'Go back to the S Bar 7 and round up the rest of the boys. This time I'll make darned certain nothing goes wrong.'

His next snappy command was aimed at Foxy Janus. 'Is it right you were a scout for the army after your trapping days fizzled out?'

An eager nod from the ageing mountain man, and he launched into what was meant to be a colourful description of his hunting adventures in Grand Teton country. His eyes misted over at the thought of those wild shindigs at the annual Green River rendezvous. 'Boy, were those crazy times. We all met up with our stock of pelts . . .'

But Steiger was not interested. 'Some other time, Foxy,' the boss rapped, chopping off the eager beaver's idle ramblings 'We have more important matters that need sorting. I want to make sure my figuring is correct. The moment you see one of those varmints riding off to get supplies, hightail it back here pronto. We'll be ready to ride at a moment's notice.'

A feeling of optimism swept through the gloomy confines of the Burning

Bush. Steiger had promised substantial bonuses to all his men once the whole valley was in his hands.

8

Possession

The three newcomers had just crested a rise that overlooked the top end of the Nueces Valley. They paused to take in the sight. Ben in particular was eager to view the land of which he was now a legal half-owner. So this is what all the hassle was about, he mused.

The cluster of buildings that made up the heart of the Jaybird holding was mainly constructed from rough-hewn logs. Nothing here was remotely attractive or pleasing to the eye. Only the barn looked in good shape, being constructed from sawn timber planking with a sloping Dutch roof. The stable, crop store and various lean-tos were huddled around the main cabin and were built to serve a practical purpose. The living quarters especially looked as if they had been thrown together by some careless giant, identifiable only because one end was of stone with a wide chimneybreast.

The entire homestead was enclosed by a pitch-pine fence and backed up against rising ground from which the infant Nueces River emerged on one side. Thundering down from the heights above in a series of rocky cascades, the water had been dammed up to provide regular irrigation for the crops during the long dry season. This innovation was what had enabled the Jaybird to thrive. That was certainly a measure to strike a positive note. Chico Lafferty clearly knew his stuff when it came to farming the land.

Behind the homestead, bare stumps indicating from where the building wood had been obtained only served to emphasize the bleak aspect. Above this, a sheer cliff face of orange sandstone rose over three hundred feet piercing the azure sky. The sound of meadowlarks and bluebirds trilling in innocence helped to convey a certain homeliness to the workaday atmosphere.

'Some spectacle, eh, you guys?' Gus

Ordway proclaimed, clearly more stimulated than Ben. 'You can see now why old Chico is so keen to prevent a takeover.' Both his new pals nodded dutifully, allowing Gus to lead the way down a winding track in single file to enter the corral at ground level through an open gate.

The moment of arrival was shattered by a large wolfhound emerging from the barn. A hostile growl was made all the more chilling due to the rat gripped between slavering pincer-like jaws. The dog's sudden appearance certainly had the desired effect of keeping the unfamiliar intruders from approaching any closer. Its purpose there was clearly to act as a deterrent. And it had worked.

Once again, Ordway proved his worth by gently cajoling the snarling beast. In no time at all, softly spoken words of reassurance had persuaded the surly beast that they were here as friends. A stick of jerky helped to seal the truce. Ben couldn't help wondering where the dog had been during the abduction of its master. Perhaps it was an easy pushover where food was involved.

With the suspect ally added to their small force, Curly Bill gave his unfettered opinion of the austere spread. 'Lafferty sure don't go in for the creature comforts, do he?' he intoned, taking in the rough-hewn sprawl. Nobody disagreed. The valley head situation was idyllic, unlike the ramshackle appearance of the accommodation.

The next day was spent investigating the Jaybird holding. Ben was eager to discover what he had signed up for. The tour, conducted by Ordway, did not take long. Unlike a cattle ranch, the fields were compact and close together. Each one was separated by a track wide enough for a wagon to load up the harvested yield. In addition to the staple crop of maize, squash and rye were cultivated. There was also an apple orchard adjoining the homestead.

It was obvious even to a greenhorn farmer like Ben Chisum that he would need to hire labour to gather in these crops at harvest time. Had he taken on far more than he could handle? Having Gus Ordway along was going to prove useful in managing the place.

The big man appeared to read his thoughts. 'Don't worry none, boss. I've worked on plenty of spreads in my time. You ain't got nothing to worry about.' A beaming grin split the furrowed façade. 'Just so long as you don't object to grafting hard from dawn 'til dusk.'

Ordway's remark was delivered with serious intent. Looking at the big guy's stoic regard, Ben could readily appreciate that sodbusting came easy to the muscle-bound simpleton. That said, he was clear in his own mind that becoming a homesteader was only ever going to be a temporary measure, a means of earning some quick dough. Although ridding the Nueces Valley of its unwelcome parasites had to be his primary task, closely followed by a better acquaintance with the delightful Elsa Durham.

After inspecting the accommodation briefly, it was clear that the vigilantes had been hard at work wrecking the place after arresting the Jaybird's occupier. A thorough search of the debris revealed a distinct lack of grub and other basic necessities. 'That guy sure didn't believe on living high on the hoof,' Curly Bill advocated, lighting up a quirley. 'All I managed to find is a sack of old pinto beans and a side of dodgy bacon. We sure can't live high on that, and all I'm packing is trail grub for another three days.'

'Reckon it'll be best if'n I go stock up at Chocktaw Charlie's Trading Post,' Ordway suggested. 'It's over the rim in the next valley so there'll be less chance of meeting up with any of Steiger's vigilantes. You fellas can sort the place out while I'm away.' He smiled. 'Make it habitable again.'

And so it was decided. The big man hitched up a wagon and set off on his two-day trek. After the two gunfighters had waved him off, Ben was all for getting started. 'How's about you make a start in the barn?' he suggested, walking across to the open door.

'As good as anywhere,' remarked Curly, following him inside. The hound sniffed the air before settling down in its kennel out of the midday heat. Inside the barn there was plenty of tidying up to do. Ben left his buddy to it while checking out all the other buildings. Luckily only the main cabin had been despoiled by the hanging party.

Emerging from a lean-to, he made his way across to begin the onerous task of making the cabin fit for human habitation, unaware that his every movement was being followed by the hawkish gaze of Foxy Janus. The tracker had spotted the wagon driven by Gus Ordway from a distance. It confirmed the boss's supposition that one of their adversaries would have to go for supplies.

Unfortunately, he was too far off to recognize the driver. Had he done so, the situation that followed would have been totally at variance. Janus's primary task now was to suss out the other guy's intentions before returning to Uvalde. He assumed that the sole occupant of the homestead now had to be Blue Creek Chisum.

Janus left his horse on the far side of a low knoll and cautiously made his way down through the rough amalgam of scrub vegetation and rocks. Great care was exercised so not to disturb any loose stones and reveal his presence. The notion occurred to the jasper's devious mind that he might even be able to surprise and remove the varmint from the picture.

An evil grin split his weathered contours. That would sure be a feather in his cap. The handicap he faced was being unaware that Chisum was not alone. Janus had arrived on the scene after Curly Bill had entered the barn. As far as he was concerned, that particular gunslinger was now on his way to Maverick, and only Chisum remained.

Edging closer, he was about to slip across the open ground to one side of the main cabin when a low growl assailed his sharp hearing. He froze, and just in the nick of time. A large dog stood stock still, not more than twenty feet away. The brute's acute sense of smell had detected the alien presence.

And it was looking his way.

Foxy knew that at such a distance a dog's blurred sight could only spot a moving object. With his breath held and not moving a muscle, he waited. The dog barked twice, snarling aggressively at the unseen intruder. Its hackles rose, teeth bared as it looked towards a cluster of boulders to the side of the main shack.

On hearing the canine warning, Ben emerged from the cabin to see what had aroused the animal. Gun drawn, he looked around. 'Hold up there, Buster,' he called out firmly, the hound having already been renamed by Gus Ordway. 'What's bugging you, then?' The dog responded with a couple more hefty barks before simmering down after being presented with another stick of jerky. Ben looked around. But nothing moved to arouse his suspicions. 'It's only a raccoon or skunk sneaking around that you've smelled, boy,' he reassured the animal gently.

Foxy Janus cursed under his breath. In his eagerness to gain the upper hand, he had forgotten the principal rule of scouting: remain invisible and blend into the landscape. But at least he had not been spotted, and Chisum did not suspect any chicanery, although the hound's presence put the kibosh on any chance of taking Chisum by surprise.

All he could do was play possum and keep absolutely still until the mutt's curiosity had abated. A thin veneer of sweat tracked across his brow while he waited until the gunslinger (now turned sodbuster) had returned to his task of restoration. Then he sneaked back to where he had left his horse. At least he could now report back to the boss that Chisum was at the Jaybird all on his ownsome.

This was news the boss would want to hear pronto.

9

. . . And Blockade

'So, my figuring was exactly as predicted,' Steiger congratulated himself. 'Curly Bill has gone for supplies, leaving Chisum a sitting duck.'

The gang leader rubbed his hands gleefully. He was surrounded by his men in the Burning Bush saloon. The drink was flowing as Steiger regaled his men with the financial benefits of supporting his plan for a takeover. 'We're all gonna be landowners, boys. I'll have the biggest cattle ranch in the territory run by the highest-paid hands. And after what Foxy has just told us, this time we'll make darned certain that two-bit skunk doesn't escape. You done well, Foxy,' he praised the trapper, slapping him on the back.

'There's a guard dog we'll need to get rid of,' Foxy cautioned. 'The savage brute lives in a kennel near the barn.'

Steiger was not in the least bit fazed. 'Don't worry about that. I know exactly how to remove his bite. Set 'em up again, bartender.'

The shady rancher wanted his men all fired up for the Jaybird raid. And hard liquor would make them eager for a fight, removing any inhibitions regarding personal safety. There were bound to be some casualties in a shootout involving Blue Creek Ben Chisum. Just so long as one of them was not Web Steiger.

Ten minutes later, he called a halt to the festivities. 'OK, boys, it's time we let off some fireworks. Get your horses ready and make sure to pack enough ammo. We ride in half an hour. This is gonna be a thanksgiving party like no other.'

A series of uproarious hoots rang out as the men dispersed. The more sober citizens of Uvalde might well have wondered what all the commotion was about, but they turned their heads away and carried on minding their own business. That was the best policy when Web Steiger and his crew were in town. The vigilante leader's interpretation of the law had made its mark. Only the bravest or most foolhardy, like Chico Lafferty and Amos Durham, had sought to challenge his self-appointed authority in the Nueces. And look what had happened to them.

It was an upbeat group of vigilantes that rode out of Uvalde with Steiger at their head. By his side was Squint Rizzo, who intended to be the one who fired the killing shot that would ensure his old partner caused him no more trouble in this world. What happened in the next one was of no concern to him.

Ben and his buddy were inside the main cabin when the conclave of vigilantes arrived en masse. Acting on Steiger's orders, the gang dispersed, making full use of any available cover to conceal their presence. No point in warning the alleged trespasser that he was under surveillance.

Inside the cabin, the new owner of the Jaybird and his pal were making do with fatback and beans cooked over an open fire in the large grate that dominated the main room of the shack. It was the smoke billowing from the chimney that had alerted Steiger to the occupation of the cabin.

The simple meal would suffice until such time as Gus Ordway returned. 'Steiger ain't gonna sit quiet and allow us to control the shots,' Redleg remarked while chewing on a piece of hard bacon. 'When do you figure he'll make another attempt to frighten us off?'

Ben considered the notion. 'That trick we pulled in Sidewinder Gulch will have shaken the skunks up. It'll give us some breathing space. Reckon while Gus is away we ought to go visit some of the other homesteads in the valley,' he suggested. 'Try and persuade them to back us in a fight against Steiger.' He took a sip of coffee to wash down the rancid bacon. 'But not before we've finish this splendid meal you cooked up.'

A grimacing face, however, told a different story that elicited a spirited rejoinder from Curly. 'It ain't that bad. A sight better than having to eat that dead cat Jennison shot for us after we'd fled Charlottesville. Boy, that sure was an all-time low. I can still taste it.' He hawked out a piece of fat into the fire.

'Guess you're right there, pal,' Ben chuckled, acknowledging the reminder. 'This is a foodie feast by comparison.' He was leaning across to refill his coffee mug when the all-too-familiar shout of Web Steiger's stentorian voice pierced the heavy log walls of the cabin. 'I know you're in there, Chisum. Me and my boys have gotten the cabin surrounded.' The vigilante boss paused to allow the dire warning and its consequences to have the inevitable effect.

The two men looked at each other. Neither had expected such a quick retaliation. It was a stark shock to the system. Ben's proposal of canvassing support for a counter-uprising was now redundant. Yet, always the professionals, they immediately cast off any alarm to meet this unexpected danger.

Guns were palmed as they hustled over

130

to the single glassless window. Peering out cautiously, all they could see were a dozen horses way over behind the barn. All of the invaders were hidden from view. And there, in the middle of the corral, lay the body of the wolfhound.

'Looks like Steiger ain't bluffing, Ben,' Curly remarked. 'And they've nobbled Buster with poisoned meat. What we gonna do about it?'

Before his pal could offer the vital miracle that was going to turn the tables on their antagonists, Steiger continued with his grim declaration. 'Your lookout was a pushover, Chisum. My advice is to surrender while you're still able. I promise you'll get a fair trial . . .'

Ben's anger at being wrong-footed by the wily land-grabber instigated a cutting piece of invective. 'If'n that's what you call vigilante law, I'd sooner take my chances in here and go down fighting.'

A raucous bout of ugly laughter echoed around the enclosure. 'And that's exactly what's gonna happen if'n you don't come out pronto. I know that you're alone in there and that your buddy, Redleg, has gone for supplies. But he won't get far. Don't play the hero, Blue Creek. This is your last chance. So what's it gonna be: a chance to walk away, or a futile death? You have one minute to decide.'

Silence thick as son-of-a-gun stew descended over the Jaybird. The participants could almost hear the ominous ticking of destiny's clock winding down remorselessly. But that final announcement from Steiger had brought a morsel of hope to the besieged duo. 'He obviously doesn't cotton that Gus has thrown in with us.' Curly asserted. 'Or that I'm in here as well.'

'We're still in one hell of a pickle, buddy, but at least it gives us a slight edge, if nothing else.' Ben held his partner's rigid gaze. 'Are you for surrendering . . . or do we fight it out?'

Curly's response was to check his handgun. 'I've gotten one loaded revolver and a dozen shells in my belt. What about you?'

'Reckon I'm about the same. But I did

find this old Spencer in the back room. And there's a box full of cartridges with it.' Ben hefted the well-oiled rifle, slotting a shell into the breech. The Spencer had always been well regarded. It was a reliable weapon with an efficient loading method centred on the easily thumbed hammer.

'They served us well during the war,' Curly remarked approvingly. 'Reckon it'll give these critters a hot reception as well.'

Ben nodded his agreement, moving across to the small window from where he delivered a scything reply to the vigilante's ultimatum. Swede Larson, overconfident with a twelve-to-one advantage, had failed to remove his hat while peering over the bed of the wagon.

Ben smiled to himself, taking careful aim with the rifle. The gun responded perfectly. The Swede's hat lifted skywards, his head being quickly withdrawn from view. Such was the fast-loading capacity of the Spencer that another bullet struck the drifting hat, sending it spinning off into the distance. 'There's your reply, Steiger. Now come and dig me out if'n you've gotten the nerve to try.' A guttural bout of acerbic guffawing was intended to convey a confident defiance. Inside, however, Ben's guts were a churning maelstrom of apprehension.

Steiger was in no way overawed by the defender's blasé attitude. He had the advantage of a larger force and time on his side. 'You asked for it, mister. And now you're gonna get it. OK, boys, let's blast this critter out of existence.'

A rapid salvo of gunfire erupted from the raiders. Their bullets were aimed at the thin wood of the door and the open window. Both defenders ducked as hot lead smashed their way through the aperture, splintering the door and crashing into the back wall. The incessant assault continued for two minutes, unceasing. There was little chance for the defenders to reply, such was the fury of the offensive.

The noise inside the cabin was deafening as myriad shells slammed into the walls. Both men, however, did manage

134

to get off a few shots in reply. Curly had located a narrow gun port adjacent to the door, giving him a relatively safe place from which to return fire. They were thus able to concentrate their shots at the puffs of smoke indicating where the attackers were secreted.

Following the initial barrage, Steiger called out a halt. Within seconds, a palpable silence descended over the battle zone. Any wildlife in the vicinity had long since fled to the safety of burrows and holes. A light breeze dispersed the dense cloud of gun smoke quickly.

'You still breathing, Chisum?' the upbeat vigilante hollered.

Ben's answer was a well-aimed shot that chipped fragments from the boulder behind which Steiger was sheltering, forcing him to duck down. The near miss was shrugged off, but it had made him aware that this guy would be no easy target.

Notwithstanding, he still maintained a relaxed persona. 'We can go on like this all day if'n needs be,' he called out.

'Give up now and save yourself from a violent end. You know it makes sense.'

Ben smiled at his partner before replying. The frowning scowl was full of vitriolic daring. 'And end up swinging from the end of rope? I don't think so. You've done your worst and I'm still here. What you figure on doing when the sun goes down?' A macabre bout of chuckling was enough to inform the vigilante boss of the defender's plan.

Steiger gritted his teeth. He had no intention of allowing this critter to slip away under the cloak of darkness. 'OK, boys,' he ordered. 'Start moving in. I want this critter winkled out, pronto.'

Moments later, the attack resumed, this time with a far greater intensity as the vigilantes crept forward. Bullets by the dozen thudded into the ugly yet solidly built structure. Many of them penetrated small gaps and apertures. Thankfully, thus far, none had struck their intended targets. Both incumbents fully appreciated that could only be a matter of time.

Yet all did not go the attackers' way: the

heavy broadside could only be carried out by exposing themselves to counter fire. Ben spotted a tall lanky jasper emerging from behind a lean-to with the aim of reaching a water trough. Stringbean never made it before being cut down by a fifty-calibre shell from the Spencer.

First blood to the defenders.

Another who tried sneaking round the side of the cabin was spotted by Redleg through a gap in the door. He pulled it open and shot the assailant through the heart — but not without perilous consequences. The gambit had exposed him to retaliation, which came in the form of a deadly barrage. Before he had chance to close the door, two slugs bit deep into soft flesh. Curly Bill cried out, tumbling back into the cabin. Ben left the window quickly and hurried across, slamming the door shut.

'They got me, pard, in the leg and stomach.' Ben helped his pal into a chair and quickly tied both of their neckers around the wound to staunch the blood.

'It ain't too bad,' Ben established,

although his voice lacked conviction. 'I'll keep them busy until nightfall, then we'll scarper.'

'You ready to surrender now, Blue Creek?' Curly Bill's sudden appearance had clearly been too quick for him to be identified by the assailants. In spite of everything, Steiger was still under the impression that only one man was holed up in the cabin. 'You can't last out much longer.'

Ben hustled across to the small aperture. 'It's only a flesh wound, Steiger. You'll have to do a sight better than that.' He pumped a couple of rounds in the general direction of the attackers to demonstrate his unwillingness to back down.

* * *

The gang boss was fuming. This guy was like the cat with nine lives. How was he going to dig the critter out? It was Squint Rizzo who provided the answer.

Here was the hired gunman's chance

to get back in the boss's good books. They had pulled this stunt a couple of times successfully during the war. There was no reason it shouldn't work here.

10

Despair . . .

'There's a wagon full of straw inside the barn,' he advocated briskly. 'All it needs is setting alight and four men to push it up alongside the blank wall of the cabin. I'll take charge. With full covering fire, we can back off without being caught in the open.' He pointed out an extra flourish that would seal the fate of the skunk inside the cabin. 'And we'll use lighted torches to toss onto the dry sod roof. That'll fix him good and proper.'

The proposal received a gloating smirk. 'Good thinking, Squint.' A gleam of triumph glinted in Steiger's eye. 'Get to it, boys. Let's burn this critter out.' The furious bombardment faded as the new plan was put into operation. Ten minutes later, the wagon emerged through the open barn door. Rizzo had fashioned a couple of torches soaked in tallow fat. He handed one to Buckshot Roberts.

The wagon was pushed up alongside the sidewall of the cabin and the straw set alight. In no time, it became a roaring inferno. Backing off, Rizzo and Roberts tossed their burning torches onto the roof, adding to the conflagration.

It was not long before smoke began drifting through the walls of the cabin. A crackling and spluttering from the roof was enough to inform the two occupants that the fire was consuming the dry turf eagerly. The writing was on the wall. How much longer could they hold out?

Ben's pal was badly injured, more so than he had initially grasped, and they were both down to their last few cartridges. Reading his thoughts, Curly made his decision. He knew the score. He struggled to his feet, swaying drunkenly. But there was a solid determination, evident in his stoical gaze, to go out with a bang. 'I've only gotten three shells left, Ben.' Pain was evident in the garbled announcement. 'My days are numbered.' His breathing was shallow and laboured. 'And I ain't about to waste

141

them. At least you have a chance to save yourself if'n you sneak out back. Now get going while I hold them off.'

Even as they conversed, the upper boards holding the sod roof began to collapse inwards. The cabin was filling with smoke rapidly. Ben gripped his partner's hand. His head fell onto his chest to hide the anguish gripping his soul. Tears dribbled down through the stubble of his cheeks. He hated leaving, but it was the only way. 'I'll make darned sure to avenge what Steiger is doing,' he promised.

Curly was already moving towards the door. Ben turned away, entering the back room where he was just able to squeeze through a tiny aperture. Outside, he scrambled up the slope, keeping low and taking cover behind jutting rocks and tree stumps. Inside the cabin, two shots rang out. A cry from out front educed a tight-lipped smile. At least Curly had made one of his bullets count.

He zigzagged further up the slope, taking advantage of stunted bushes while aiming for the base of the cliff above.

Following a cessation of hostilities, it was clear that the fire-raisers were enjoying the success of their macabre display.

At that moment a single shot rang out from inside the cabin. Now fully alight, orange tongues of flame began to feast on the timber banquet quickly. Smoke was beginning to obscure the homestead. Ben's face creased up. A blend of torment and hatred warped the handsome façade. His friend had made the ultimate sacrifice before the flames finished their gruesome handiwork.

For a brief moment Ben was stricken by grief. Escape was the only way to even the score. He shook the mush from his head, resuming his scramble up towards the rocky enclave. Thankfully, his breakout had gone unnoticed. Nobody was following. All their attention was focused on the conflagration. It did not elude his thinking that one body, burnt to a crisp and unidentifiable, would convince Web Steiger that Blue Creek Ben Chisum had been eliminated from the fray.

And that was going to be his ace in

the pack.

On reaching the bottom of the cliff face, some two hundred feet above the elliptical amphitheatre enclosing the homestead, he was forced to stop. Pausing to regain his breath, he could just make out the outline of the burning buildings below. But there was no cover up here to hide behind once the smoke dispersed.

Had he merely traded one trap for another? A search along the base revealed no way forward. He was stuck. There was no way out. And when the smoke finally cleared he would be in full view of fire-raisers below. Panic gripped his innards, threatening to engulf the normally cool disposition. Surely having eluded the grim reaper's swinging scythe he would not be stymied at this crucial stage. A brief prayer for salvation was despatched to a God he had too long ignored.

Awaiting the onset of darkness, a factor he had hoped to exploit earlier, was now a closed book. The fire was likely to burn all through the night, providing sufficient illumination for the vigilantes to spot an escaping fugitive easily. Equally grim was the certainty they would stick around to ensure the burnt-out cabin contained a body.

That notion produced yet another unwelcome assumption in the trapped man's disturbed brain. Rather than go after the man bringing in supplies, Steiger was astute enough to wait below and ambush the unwary Gus Ordway when he arrived back. And then the cat would be well and truly out of the bag. Steiger would know that Ordway had joined up with the two gunslingers. And that meant they both must have been inside the cabin when it was attacked. So where was the other body?

All of these hair-raising notions flitted through Ben Chisum's fizzing brain. Somehow he had to find a way out of this dilemma. A furious desperation lent new vigour to his hunt for a way out. But either end of the cliff was blocked by an abrupt downfall. There was no means of reaching the open sward below anyway. And climbing the vertical rock wall was way beyond his capabilities.

Just when he had given up hope, his foot slipped into a hole at the base of the cliff. It was covered by a low bunch of scrub vegetation. Clawing the thorny branches aside, he uncovered a small aperture wide enough for a man to climb into. A renewed sense of optimism surged through Ben's tired frame as he lowered himself gingerly into the dark entrance. There he paused, adjusting his vision to the pitch-blackness. By feeling his way along the rough wall, it soon became clear he was inside the entrance to a mining adit.

Delving fingers scrabbling blindly around were fortunate enough to locate a discarded torch. He struck a vesta on the wall and applied it. The flickering light revealed a tunnel driving into the mountainside. It was supported by wooden beams. His assumption had been right. And there on the floor were three sacks. Could this be what he thought it was?

Tentatively, he opened a bag. A stunned gasp hissed out from between gritted teeth, a quickening of the heart. The pale light emphasized streaks of glittering yellow. Ben's staring eyes bulged wide, barely able to credit what he was seeing.

Gold! No man is immune from the tempting allure engendered by the yellow peril. Not even Ben Chisum. Trembling hands caressed the nobbly chunks of ore. Then it all fell into place. Web Steiger must have found out that there was gold on Jaybird land. That was the reason he was so eager to take control. He had concealed the entrance to the mine until such time as the ore could be extracted. All that blarney about bringing law to the Nueces Valley was a front to conceal his true motive.

This was one more reason why Ben had to find a way out. But there was his stumbling block. How did finding the mineshaft help him with that quest? He slumped down, struggling to hold off the wave of despair threatening to drown

147

him. His old pal gone, and the simple nester Gus Ordway heading for the same roundup.

And then there was Elsa Durham. This was the first time since their parting that he had been able to give her more than a passing thought. Was it only a couple of days ago? It seemed like weeks had gone by. He knew that something had passed between them, a spark of passion, a tender feeling alien to the hard-bitten gunfighter, but one he now valued more than anything. Was that to be blown away like grains of desert sand?

He shook off the bleak despondence. This was no time to be consumed by self-pity. Ben Chisum had always found a way out of his difficulties.

Scrambling to his feet, he moved further down the tunnel. Water dribbled from the roof barely a few inches above his head. And it was becoming steadily narrower, forcing him to bend low. The torch was also losing its strength rapidly. Perhaps he should abandon the search. No sooner had that unsettling notion entered his head when the torch fizzled and died.

The horror at being entombed had to be fought off. Eyes clamped tight shut, he forced his brain to remain calm. Such had been the strain of the last few hours that exhaustion claimed Ben's whacked frame.

How long he remained in the arms of Morpheus was impossible to say. Suddenly, his eyes flickered open. For a moment, his brain failed to register his predicament. Then it struck home like the kick from a loco mule. He might well have succumbed to ultimate despair, had a brief waft of cool air not caressed his cheek. Suddenly reanimated, he scrambled to his feet. It was coming from his left along a side passage.

11

. . . And Deliverance

His heart quickened this time in expectation of deliverance from this nightmare. As he neared the end of the passage, the zephyr became more pronounced. Striking another vesta, he raised it above his head, revealing a narrow flue striking upwards that confirmed his conjecture. The near-vertical chimney was narrow, but just wide enough for a lean-limbed jigger to negotiate with care.

Flexing his hands, he breathed deep and began the tenuous ascent. Luckily, there were plenty of handholds and footholds to assist the climb; but it was all in pitch darkness, thick as treacle, so every step had to be tested. Sharp outcrops of rock scraped his exposed flesh, drawing blood. The pain was ignored. Only the thought of reaching open ground above occupied his thoughts now.

The going was slow in the extreme,

but at least he was making progress, and with each foot gained, the exit from this living nightmare drew closer.

Then, all at once, his head banged against the roof of the chimney. Blood dribbled down into his eyes. Open or shut made no difference. He cried out. A raised arm blindly searching told him that the chimney had veered to the right. For a brief moment he became stuck.

Bending sideways, he forced his hand around the obstruction, fingers scrabbling for a hold. Sweat poured off his face. A surge of nausea swept over him. Wriggling like an angry rattler, skinned and bleeding fingers finally managed to drag him around the obstruction. Tortured lungs dragged in huge gulps of life-enhancing oxygen. He paused to regain his breath before pushing on up the chimney. Passing round the constriction revealed a round disc of light above.

'Thank you,' he murmured to his maker before anger took precedence. 'I'm gonna make you pay big time for this, Steiger,' he blurted out aloud as a fresh wave of energy enabled him to press onward. Not far to go now. The aperture was now a gaping hole no more than fifteen feet above.

But the physical demands on his body were exhausting. After resting a moment to allow his head to clear, the climb was resumed with infinite concentration. And ten minutes later he was lying spread-eagled on the hard ground above, gasping for air like a landed trout.

Time had passed quickly. Darkness had quickly spread its stygian tentacles across the rough terrain. Overhead the silvery disc beamed down, bathing the relieved fugitive in its ethereal glow. It was a beacon of hope, a sign of deliverance, a message from the heavens amidst the patchwork of twinkling sequins.

Ben heaved himself up on to his knees. Hands were clasped together, head bowed in prayer. 'I won't never take you for granted again, Lord,' he promised. At that moment, it was a heartfelt vow. He had been given a second chance. Would he be able to profit from such a miracle?

He peered over the rim of the mesa. Down below, the spluttering crackle of burning timber could be heard. Sore eyes failed to spot any movement. But he knew they were down there, scavenging predators waiting to pounce on the unsuspecting Gus Ordway. There was no time to lose if Ben was to save his new partner.

Light from the moon together with the glow of the conflagration provided sufficient light for him to pick a tenuous path down through broken terrain. The lower he descended, the more care was needed to avoid revealing his presence. It was vital that he secure a horse.

Nearing the homestead, he became aware of a campfire burning on the edge of the clearing. Men were sat round, shovelling grub down their gullets while staring hypnotically at the inferno they had created. They were laughing and joking, egged on by that skunk Rizzo.

Secure in the knowledge that the occupant of the cabin had been incinerated, Steiger had not bothered to post a guard. As a result, it was easy for Ben to locate his own horse and coax it away quietly from the others with gentle whisperings of well-being.

It was with a huge sigh of relief, mixed with heartache, that he walked the animal back into the secure blanket of darkness. Mounting up at a safe distance, he rode away, swearing to avenge the destruction of life and property rained down on him by Web Steiger and his bunch of self-styled vigilantes.

He headed off in the general direction taken by Gus Ordway. Soon, his head was drooping onto his chest as fatigue threatened to overcome him. The desperate climb up the chimney had taken its toll. Rest was needed urgently if he was not to fall out of the saddle. A small glade hidden from view within a clump of palo verde trees offered safety for what remained of the night. Luckily, his saddle pack had not been touched. In a daze, he wrapped himself in the bedroll and was asleep in moments. Only an earthquake would have brought him round.

Dawn had come and gone. The sun was well above the horizon, beaming down on the comatose huddle lying in the open glade. It was a deer tugging at the saddle blanket that brought the sleeping figure back to life. The animal scampered away in fright. Ben was awake in moments, unsure where he was.

Then it all came back, striking hard like a sucker punch in the guts. The battle, the fire, the sacrifice of his old friend. Not to mention the discovery of the hidden mine, and the final nightmare crawl to freedom up that twisting flue. But was he safe? Had those critters discovered Curly Bill's remains? And what of Gus Ordway? Would he be in time to prevent another miscarriage of justice? Such questions flooded his turgid brain. But of answers there were none.

He stumbled to his feet, grabbing the water bottle and tipping the contents over his head. A deep draught also helped to return him to something resembling normality, if that would ever be the same again. Packing up quickly, he was soon on the trail. An hour's riding later and he spotted the turn-off where the wagon had left the main trail. This had to be the route Ordway had taken.

Climbing steadily up into the foothills through dense stands of pine, it was late afternoon before he spotted a wagon heading towards him. Tightly strung nerves could now relax knowing he had found the guy. Another prayer of thanksgiving was despatched aloft.

'Boy, am I glad to see you,' he hollered when they finally met up.

Ordway's laggard brain was thrown into confusion. 'What you doing out here, boss?' he asked, hauling the team to a halt. But he was not so simple as to recognize all was not well at the Jaybird. 'Some'n bad happened?'

'Couldn't be much worse, pal,' Ben blurted out, struggling to contain his anguish. 'Curly's dead and the homestead has gone up in flames.' Barely pausing to draw breath, he hurried on. All his sup-pressed anger gushed forth as he described the lurid details of the attack and its aftermath.

'I ought never to have gone over the divide for them supplies,' Gus berated himself, feeling guilty at having abandoned his new pals. 'I should have been there fighting alongside of you.'

Ben's anger-tinged features softened as he laid a commiserating hand on the big man's shoulder. 'Don't whip yourself, Gus. Nobody reckoned on Steiger getting there so fast. If'n anyone's to blame, it has to be me for not taking the critter seriously enough.'

Both men sunk into a torpid morass of gloom. Sat facing each other, each was cocooned in his own morbid thoughts. It was Ben who broke in on the despondent lassitude. 'When the fire has burned itself out, those skunks will only find one body and they'll think it's me.' A smile lacking any hint of levity drew warped furrows of vengeful bile that had even a tough *hombre* like Gus Ordway quaking in his boots. 'And that's gonna be our saving grace. I'm determined to scupper that no-account's plan to take over this valley, or die in the trying.'

One aspect of the recent debacle he made sure to keep firmly locked inside his head was the discovery of the hidden gold mine. He had only known Gus Ordway a short time. The fella seemed genuine enough, but there was no denying that he was a bullet short of a full chamber. A loose tongue in the wrong ear could lead to unwanted trouble. And he had enough of that on his plate already.

Gus picked up on his pard's resurrected optimism. 'And I'll be with you all the way, boss,' he averred with vigorous intent. 'So where to now?'

'We need to get over to the Durham spread,' was the brisk reply. 'I have to make sure Elsa is OK. Steiger has given her notice to quit. And that could happen any day unless we work out some kind of plan to stall him.'

Whipping up the horse-drawn wagon, Gus led the way across country. He knew of another less well-used trail that would avoid any likelihood of meeting up with the opposition. Part of the route took them through Rattlesnake Gulch. On this occasion there was no elation, no letting off steam at having thwarted the opposition. The full horror, the guilt at having failed his partner, now washed over Ben Chisum. He was relieved when they emerged on the far side.

For the next hour they rode in silent contemplation. Ordway cast numerous pensive looks at his associate. Each time he tried to broach the subject of their future strategy, the grim regard held him back. Black eyebrows met in the middle of Ben's forehead. Only a slight tic above his left eye indicated that the gunfighter's brain was hard at work.

Only when they were approaching the Durham homestead did Ben manage to cast off the lethargic melancholy that had stuck to him like glue. And the reason for his rejuvenation was the presence of two horses outside the cabin. They might well be merely friends visiting. There again, they could be messengers sent by Steiger to issue a final warning on the eviction.

An innate caginess cultivated over the years made him hang back, and just in time as two hard-nosed jaspers emerged from the cabin. Ben recognized them as the pair he had questioned in Maverick when first trying to find Amos Durham.

Laredo and his buddy Bug Pincher wandered over to where their horses were tethered. Laredo turned back. His hectoring tone carried back to the newcomers hidden behind the barn. 'You make sure to be out of here by Sunday, lady, else the boss will be none too pleased.'

'That's only three days off. I need more time,' she pleaded.

'There's been enough stalling already,' rasped Laredo. 'Sunday, or it'll be the worse for you.'

Elsa's shoulders slumped in despair. Standing on the veranda, her dejected expression melted Ben's heart and made him want to leap out and confront this odious pair of bullyboys. Gus Ordway instantly read his mind. A powerful hand gripped him tightly.

'Don't reckon that would be a smart move, boss,' he whispered, anticipating his partner's reckless intention astutely. 'Secrecy is on our side. Let's keep it that way. They still figure you're dead and that Curly is the only one left. And by now they'll likely figure he's skipped the territory. If'n those two critters fail to report back, Steiger will be alerted to the fact that his plan has somehow gone wrong.'

Ben struggled but was no match for the bruiser's muscle power. But a new-found look of respect was aimed his way. 'You're one smart cookie, Gus. Guess I wasn't thinking straight.' The big man brightened under the unfamiliar acclaim. Only when the messengers had rode off did they emerge from hiding and hurry across to where Elsa was slumped in a chair on the porch.

She quaked on hearing their approach. Only when she recognized Ben and Gus did she lurch to her feet. In a moment she was in his arms, tears streaming down her cheeks. 'They said you were likely dead by now,' the girl stuttered out, grateful that the awful news was clearly false. 'And that Chico would be next.'

'They were nearly right,' Ben replied holding her close. 'But the Jaybird has gone up in smoke and a pal who helped me out from the old days paid with his life.' He extricated himself gingerly from Elsa's fearful grasp. 'I was wrong to figure on scotching Steiger's plan on my ownsome.'

'So it's all over. Is that what you're saying?' The girl's belligerent accusation was more of anger at Web Steiger than anyone else.

'Not while I'm still drawing breath, it ain't,' he asserted firmly. 'You're well respected by all the homesteaders in the valley. Can you arrange a secret meeting of all those you can trust? I have a plan that might turn the tables on the skunk once and for all.'

A fresh look of hope brought colour into the girl's cheeks. 'You really think we can beat him?' A firm nod of accord saw her agreeing to his proposal avidly. 'I'll have Obediah Crawley spread the word among the others. We can all meet up in his quarters back of the blacksmith's workshop.'

'Sooner the better. I need to go find Chico. I have a special job that will suit him perfectly. So make it Saturday morning. Two days should give us enough time to get this shindig on the move.'

'What part do I play in all this?' Gus enquired.

'The most important job of all.' Ben's face assumed an earnest look. 'I need for you to stay with Elsa in case those critters come back and start making trouble for her. Think you can handle it?'

The big guy squared his shoulders. 'Anyone tries forcing their way in here will get a belly full of lead.'

12

Baiting the Trap

Ben rode all through the night and most of the next day to reach Del Rio, only stopping to snatch a few hours sleep. When he reached the sleepy town, his first call was at the office of the attorney who had prepared the deed of land ownership for the Jaybird. The man was loath to disclose where his client was staying.

'I don't know,' the man declared somewhat reluctantly. 'Mister Lafferty was adamant that his hiding place should remain secret until the trouble with the vigilantes has been settled.'

But Ben was nothing if not persuasive, assuring the reticent official that contacting the homesteader was a matter of life and death. 'I'm his partner, as designated on the agreement, and it's vital that I speak with him. He sure won't thank you for refusing to disclose his whereabouts when he eventually finds out what I have to tell him, and by then it will be too late.'

After some more desultory hesitation, the lawyer finally agreed to the request. 'You won't regret it, Mister Harker,' Ben assured the worried man after being given directions to the home of Lafferty's cousin.

Pedro Gonzalez lived in a small shack in the foothills above Del Rio where he ran a small chicken farm supplying eggs to the local townships. Without the detailed instructions supplied by the lawyer, he would never have found the place. Chico had chosen his hideout well.

When the log cabin came into view, he paused. It sat in a hollow surrounded by trees and was virtually impossible to locate by the unwary. The only means of identifying its location was a splintered rock known as the Devil's Knitting Needle. Riding straight in without any warning might well earned him a bullet from a man living on his nerves. He moved in as close as possible without revealing his presence. And there he waited impatiently for somebody to emerge.

Ten minutes passed before the door opened, and a corpulent peon came out with a bucket and began tossing feed into the enclosure containing at least fifty hens. Ben waited for him to finish before edging closer and stepping out into the open. 'Señor Gonzalez, don't be afraid,' he whispered urgently, holding his hands high. 'I come in peace to see my partner, Chico.'

The shock made the Mexican drop the bucket. His mouth hung open as he staggered back in terror. Ben quickly made to reassure the frightened man that he meant him no harm. 'Chico said that if I ever needed to contact him, I should come here, and what I have to tell him is of the utmost importance. Is he still living here with you?'

'It is all right, Pedro,' a quiet voice announced from the doorway of the cabin. 'This is the man who saved me from being lynched by Web Steiger and his gang. I owe him my life.' His next remark was for the surprise visitor. 'Something big must have happened to bring you all the way out here, Ben.'

'Can we go inside, pard?' he said as tiredness from his hectic journey and the recent gun battle suddenly claimed his shattered frame. He reeled drunkenly, eyes rolling up inside his head. 'I'm plumb . . . tuckered out,' he grunted, 'and could sure use . . . a cup of strong coffee. I've rode all the way . . . from the Durham place.'

Chico hurried forward, urging his cousin to help him get the exhausted man inside the cabin.

How long Ben was out cold he could only guess at. When he finally surfaced, it was dark outside and he was splayed out on a grubby cot. The dim glow cast by a smoky oil lamp was the sole form of illumination inside the cabin.

'H-how long have I b-been out?' he stammered, bleary eyes trying to focus in the diffused light.

Chico immediately helped his partner sit up. 'A full twelve hours. You needed the rest. The body can only take so much, then it shuts down.'

Ben struggled to get up, but Chico and his cousin held him back. 'I need to be getting back to Uvalde,' he pressed. 'There's gonna be a secret meeting I arranged to see what can be done to defeat Steiger.'

'Not so fast, *amigo*,' Chico cautioned, holding a cup containing a vile smelling concoction to Ben's lips. 'Drink this. It is a special family brew passed down through generations of our family. It will make you feel better.'

Ben's nose wrinkled. But he managed to down the nauseating concoction without vomiting. It tasted worse than it looked. But within minutes he could feel the energy flowing back into his wasted muscles. 'Boy, you ain't wrong there, Chico. That stuff sure packs a punch.'

'You still need to rest a couple more hours to allow it to work properly,' Chico advised. 'In the meantime, how about you tell why you sought me out?'

Before Ben could launch into his

macabre tale, Pedro stuck a bowl of chicken broth in front of him. 'A man needs to keep his strength up when he has dealt with death and destruction like you have, *señor*.' The farmer's shrewd counsel elicited a nod of approval from his cousin, who pushed a hunk of bread into his hand.

'Pedro is right,' Chico concurred. 'No man can keep going on empty stomach for too long. Eat up, is very good.'

Although it looked no better than the elixir, Ben shrugged and proceeded to empty the bowl. He soon wolfed it down, offering no complaint. Indeed, it was the best and only meal he had eaten since first leaving Elsa Durham, which now seemed like the distant past. The bacon and beans in the old cabin didn't count.

With his strength returning rapidly, Ben proceeded to relate the full horror of what had occurred at the Jaybird in all its gory detail. A glint of understanding appeared in the half-breed's eyes when the discovery of gold on his land was revealed. But it was not the avaricious leer that affected most *hombres* after discovering they have struck it rich.

Chico was more concerned about the burning out of his property and the death of Curly Bill Redleg. 'So, now it becomes clear why that skunk wanted Jaybird land. He must have uncovered an entrance to the mine on the far side of the mountain and followed it through.' He stood up and walked over to a black pot simmering on a stove and poured himself a cup of coffee.

After a few minutes concentrated assimilation of this unsettling news, he turned back, having come to a decision. 'I'm getting too long in the tooth to be bothered with all the riches gold can buy,' he declared firmly, yet with measured circumspection. 'If'n we come out of this fracas on the winning side, I want to do some good with it. Turn the valley into a thriving settlement, a place for folks to live in peace. Steiger has driven a lot of good people out. Greed has been at the heart of all his weasel words about bringing law to the territory.'

His eyes rested on his associate, issuing a challenge to dispute his altruistic objective. 'So, what is your view, Ben Chisum?'

Ben had been considering his reply and now carefully delivered his verdict. 'At one time, I'd have been glassy-eyed at the life of luxury stretching out before me if'n a gold mine had landed in my lap. But having gotten myself caught up in this range war, I'm with you all the way, pal. The Nueces could become a guiding light for other parts of Texas to follow.'

Then his pragmatic nature took back control. There was still the thorny business of defeating Web Steiger's grasping ambition. 'But first, I need to get back to Uvalde before that meeting gets underway. The skunk will have concluded by now that Curly won't be coming back. Our secret ingredient is that he'll also have figured it's my charred body found in the burnt-out wreckage of the cabin.'

Chico couldn't resist a morbid chuckle of delight. 'He sure is gonna receive one almighty surprise and no mistake when he discovers the truth.'

'I'd love to see his face when the truth dawns. First, though, I need you to do something while I'm gone. Then you can come and join in the fun.'

Ben then went on to explain what he had in mind. Having explained his plan for Chico to carry out, he set off back for Uvalde. Pedro supplied him with some chicken sandwiches to stave off any pangs of hunger during the journey. Ben was mightily touched by the peon's thoughtfulness. He squeezed his shoulder. 'I'm gonna make it my business to see you set up with a proper spread to expand this enterprise once we've rid the valley of its vermin.'

He spurred off into the half-light of the false dawn, firm in his belief that he had done right in sticking with these homespun folk. But only time would tell if'n it was a wise decision. Thinking about Elsa Durham only served to confirm his belief that the Nueces Valley was where he wanted to finally settle down.

And if'n that meant tending crops and milking cows, then so be it. With the girl of his dreams to keep him warm on cold nights, what more could a retired gun-fighter want from life?

The sun was peeping over the scalloped rim of the mesa when Chico mounted up. Pedro was eager to join his cousin in the task outlined by Blue Creek Chisum, but Chico was adamant that he should go alone. 'This is my problem, *primo*,' he insisted. 'You stay here and look after the chickens. I would never forgive myself should any harm come to you.'

In his heart, Gonzalez knew he would be more of a hindrance than a help with the tricky undertaking. 'Then look after yourself, Chico. These are bad *gringos* you are tangling with.' Pedro rubbed his cousin's neck to remind him that a neck-tie party would be the price of failure. 'Next time, those *ratas* will not let you escape.'

Lafferty shrugged off the warning, but it had struck home nevertheless. A brisk nod of understanding, then he

173

rode away, leaving his cousin shaking his head with ominous foreboding. A brisk ride lay ahead of him to reach the town of Maverick before the general business of the day brought people out onto the streets.

Two hours later, Chico sat his horse, looking down on Maverick from the cover of some juniper trees. The building he sought was on the main street. He would need to approach it from the rear to avoid being spotted. Gingerly, he nudged the horse down the tortuous narrow trail, reaching the back entrance safely. Nervous eyes panned the immediate vicinity of the Del Rio vigilante office.

What Ben Chisum had in mind would make those critters sit up and take notice. A satisfying grin cracked the swarthy face. An eye for an eye was nothing if not a fitting payback. One final look around and Chico hustled across to the back door. He stuck an iron bar into the gap near the lock and heaved. It was only a plank door, not designed to withstand any serious assault. A splintering crack soon found the lock breaking loose.

He slipped inside quickly, unloading the goods he had brought to complete his mission of destruction. The two bottles of tallow oil were splashed around. No further time was wasted as a scratched vesta was applied to an oily rag. Backing across to the open door, he tossed it into the room. The result was instantaneous. A whoosh followed as the fire caught the soaked woodwork. Flames leaped across the floor, eagerly devouring everything in their path.

This was no time to linger in admiration of his handiwork. He dashed out of the building and across to where his horse was tethered. But he was not alone. Two of Steiger's men had arrived early to open up the premises. Their job was to administer any so-called law enforcement deemed necessary to provide a cover for the vigilante leader's true intentions. It also helped to establish a *bona fide* presence in the valley.

Smoke was already drifting out of the

open door. 'Hey, Bug,' Laredo called out to his buddy. 'It looks like the office is on fire.'

Quick on the uptake, Pincher spotted the perpetrator heading across the back lot. 'Ain't that Lafferty over yonder? The skunk must have come out of hiding and decided to get his revenge by burning down the office.'

The two men grabbed for their guns. 'Hold up there, scumbag. You're under arrest,' Laredo shouted. 'Don't move, else you're a dead man.'

Shocked by this sudden interruption to his plan, Chico had no intention of surrendering to face another hanging. His hand dropped to pull his own shooter in answer to the challenge. But these were hardened gunmen. The two Navy Colts blasted apart the early morning silence. Once, twice, three times, the simultaneous reports of discharging firearms tore down the fetid silence. Black powder smoke filled the air, mingling with that of the ever more dense surge of wood smoke.

Chico Lafferty stood no chance against such a lethal detonation. His punctured body spun round, arms flailing wildly like some demented puppet, finally tumbling in a heap of bloody clothes. The killers wandered across, toeing the dead carcass idly. 'The boss will be pleased we removed this piece of trash,' Bug Pincher declared, a lascivious grin painted across his gaunt kisser.

'Like as not, we'll be up for a good bonus when he hears about it,' concurred Laredo, not in the slightest bit fazed by the sudden death-dealing action.

The gunfire had attracted other early risers to the grim scene. They just stood apart, staring at the gruesome result of vigilante law. But already the fire had grabbed a firm hold of the office, threatening to engulf other buildings nearby. Cries of alarm jolted the watchers into action.

'Fire! Fire!' Pincher shouted. 'Somebody go call out the fire brigade.' Every town in the west, however small, had some form of fire-fighting organization.

Conflagrations were the most feared hazard facing wood-framed settlements. Too many of them had gone up in smoke for the matter to be taken lightly.

Suddenly, the thought of monetary rewards faded as the two killers hurried to join in with the panic-driven rush to save the building. Luckily, it was separate from the others, so none of the other watchers were in any hurry to comply. The disappearance of the vigilante headquarters was no loss to the town.

13

Mixed Fortunes

The clandestine meeting was already assembled when Ben finally slipped in the back door of the blacksmith's shop. He could hear raised voices grumbling about having been dragged away from their businesses. It was clear that Elsa had told the gathering that the infamous gunfighter had a plan to rid the valley of Web Steiger's vigilante gang. Likewise, it was equally apparent that some members of the council were decidedly reluctant to place their future in the hands of a hired gunslinger that had once ridden with Squint Rizzo.

'What guarantee do we have that this guy ain't also in Steiger's pocket?' the town barber voiced, wiping sweat from the bald pate that had resulted in the somewhat discomfiting nickname of Egghead. 'The way I see it, a leopard never changes its spots. A guy who works for the highest bidder can't be trusted to back our interests.'

The view offered by Reubin Varney did not appear to be shared by the majority. They all respected Elsa, who had urged Obediah Crawley to summon this extraordinary council meeting. All the same, it was a vociferous minority. And they needed convincing that Ben Chisum was the only one who could bring peace back to the Nueces.

The man under fire chose that moment to step out of the shadows. 'I want Rizzo out of the way just as much as you men,' he stressed, moving into the light cast by the blacksmith's blazing fire. 'More so, seeing as he betrayed me to the *federales* down in Zaragoza.' He moved into the centre of the group, standing beside Elsa. 'You might think you are safe from Steiger's depredations here in Uvalde. But I can tell you for a fact that he's after taking over the entire valley.'

'He just wants the land to expand his cattle empire,' interjected a tall, rangy jasper clad in black. Yellowing skin stretched tight across a bony skull gave a skeletal appearance perfectly in accord with his profession, for Joseph Waldorf was the town undertaker. 'By keeping our heads down and paying for his protection, we'll be safe.'

'That ain't exactly a charitable attitude to take, Joe,' protested Mayor Crawley. 'As councillors of the main town in the Nueces Valley we have a duty of care for everybody. Too many innocent settlers have already been driven out, some even killed for objecting to Steiger's demands. I think we should at least listen to what Mister Chisum has to say before refusing his help.'

Ben chose that moment to show his hand. 'Just so that everybody knows the true reason for Steiger's land-grabbing ambition, I can tell you that it sure ain't to run more beef. The skunk couldn't give a tinker's cuss about ranching.' He paused, allowing another sceptic to question this assertion.

'If'n he ain't after more land for cattle, perhaps you could enlighten us with the real reason,' pressed Chuck Dempster, who ran the butcher's shop. It would be his business that would benefit most from increased beef sales.

Ben rolled a stogie and lit up before answering. His hawkish gaze panned across the gathering, resting for a moment on the beatific features of Elsa Durham. A hidden smile passed between them. Behind her stood the solid figure of Gus Ordway like a faithful guard dog. Ben nodded to him; he was confident she was in safe hands.

Then he delivered his eye-opening disclosure. 'Gold is what it's all about.' A sharp intake of breath heralded this shock announcement. Even Elsa was stunned by this startling revelation. 'Gold!' he repeated firmly. 'Steiger has somehow discovered a rich seam of paydirt on Jaybird land.'

Following a brief, yet noisy babble, the sceptical barber piped up. 'Maybe Lafferty knew all about it and was holding out on us 'cos he wants the whole caboodle for himself.'

Ben's face coloured with indignation.

It was a struggle to keep a tight rein on his temper. 'I've been to see Chico Lafferty,' Ben jumped in, defending his new associate vigorously. And believe me, he was a surprised as any of you. Chico doesn't want the gold for himself. He wants it to bring prosperity to the whole valley: a new hospital, running water and drainage, and a whole lot more. A place for good folks to live in peace.' He cast a challenging eye around the room. 'And those were his words, not mine.'

He paused there to allow this startling declaration to be discussed. There was certainly much to consider. The gabbling chatter was finally curtailed by the mayor clapping his hands. 'Order! Order, please, gentlemen. Allow Mister Chisum to finish his story.'

Ben terminated his rational explanation in a deadly serious manner that nobody present could mistake for levity. His voice was low, yet poignant, as he described the battle at the Jaybird homestead in lurid detail. 'Pure greed is the reason Web Steiger wants to acquire land used primarily for farming. Certainly not so he can continue growing crops there. Him and his bunch have already burned down the holding with my buddy inside. I only managed to escape by the skin of my teeth. And that's when I stumbled on the hidden mine in the hills behind. So I have every right to want that skunk brought to justice.'

More nervous muttering broke out. This altered everything. The mayor then called for a show of hands in support of his proposition to support Ben's plan of action. This time, the vote was unanimous.

'So, what have you in mind, Mister Chisum?' asked the undertaker in a far more conciliatory voice.

Ben sucked in a deep lungful of air before outlining his scheme. 'It all hangs on the citizens of this town, you men here, backing my play to the limit.' He looked round, noting the nervous glances passing between them. 'One man alone cannot defeat the vigilantes. But I can draw them into a trap from which the only escape is in a pine box if'n they choose to make a fight of it.'

'But we're shopkeepers and businessmen, not gunfighters,' the barber complained. 'You can't expect us to stand toe-to-toe with hardened *pistoleros*.'

'Just so long as you can point a gun and are pre-pared to use it, that's all I ask. You'll all be hidden from sight if Steiger falls into the trap.' Ben's measured display of confidence had certainly piqued the attention of the gathering, but there was still that vital element missing before a decision could be reached.

And it was Obediah Crawley who voiced it. 'I reckon its time we learned how Steiger is gonna be lured into this trap you've mentioned.'

Ben was ready with the answer. 'I'll need the cooperation of the newspaper editor.' All eyes swung towards Howard Nesbitt, who was still sporting his trademark eyeshade. Ben handed him a piece of paper on which he had written the contents of an advert. 'That should do the trick,' he asserted. 'Why don't you read it out, Mister Nesbitt? Then these gentlemen can judge for themselves whether it's likely to work.'

Nesbitt adjusted his spectacles before quoting the message intended for Web Steiger's scrutiny. 'Thirty hands needed to harvest crops on Jaybird land. Good pay and bonuses paid for the right men. Sign on with Ben Chisum at 10 o'clock on Thursday morning in Uvalde.'

'Reckon you can have that printed in bold on the front page of tomorrow's distribution of the *Nueces Star*?' Ben asked the somewhat bewildered newspaperman.

'Don't see why not,' was the calculated response, 'and I'll make certain that a copy is delivered to the S Bar 7 first thing.'

'So, gentlemen,' Ben said looking them each in the eye. 'That will really set the cat among the pigeons when he hears that I'm still in the land of the living. And I'll be on the main street sitting behind a table ready to sign up potential hands at the appointed time. Web

Steiger is sure to respond by riding in with all his men to ensure nobody joins me. That is the last thing he wants with all that gold up for grabs.'

'Sounds like a full blown showdown, boys,' Crawley declared to all and sundry. 'And if'n I know Steiger, there's gonna be a heap of lead flying. Are we up for it?' He swallowed to conceal his nervousness before continuing. 'I can't see any other way of defeating the critter once and for all. There must be plenty of other guys in town who feel the same and will want a part of the action. So I'm giving Ben my unqualified vote of confidence.'

One by one the others quickly nodded their heads in assent. Soon after, the meeting broke up. Before they left the blacksmith's shop, Ben issued a note of warning. 'It's vital that nobody talks about what we're planning to anybody outside this room. We don't want word getting back to Steiger. He has to be taken completely by surprise when he turns up.'

But there will always be some who can't resist a bit of gossip, especially while waiting in a barber's shop. Egghead Varney never could keep his mouth shut. Not that he had any intention of revealing the plan proposed by Ben Chisum, but the presence of gold in the valley was another thing entirely.

'Who in his right mind would ever have thought that gold would be discovered down here by Chico Lafferty?' he remarked to the man sitting in the chair, his face coated in a thick layer of shaving cream.

'Who told you about that, Egghead?' a startled patron exclaimed.

Too late, the big-mouthed barber realized that he had overstepped the mark. He quickly explained it away as the ravings of some drunk he'd bought a drink for in the saloon. 'I don't know where it is,' he hurried on eager to staunch any rumours that it was here in the Nueces. 'Could be anywhere in the state for all I know.' But his denial was not convincing.

Such a startling revelation, especially from a barber, was unlikely to be idle tittle-tattle. One man, who had only just arrived, slipped out the door quickly without uttering a word. Utah Gillick was one of Steiger's regular cowhands and he knew the boss would want to hear this news straight away.

* * *

Web Steiger was holding court in the main room of his ranch house. Sitting behind a large oak desk, a glass of best Scotch whisky in his hand, his eye glittered greedily. Laredo had just returned from Maverick. His news about the torching of the vigilante office was of no consequence in comparison to the far more noteworthy report that Lafferty had been caught in the act and shot dead.

His lip curled with the satisfaction of knowing Jaybird land was now wide open. 'All I need do is to occupy the spread and have a deed of ownership drawn up. We're almost there, boys. The

S Bar 7 is gonna be the biggest outfit in the territory with us in total command.'

Havana cigars were handed out to his most trusted cohorts, who knew that they would benefit most from the land takeover. 'Yesiree,' gushed Steiger. 'Stick with me, boys, and you'll all be living in clover. With that interfering cornball Chisum out of the way, there ain't nothing to stop us. And maybe next year we can move into Langtry County. There's a self-appointed judge called Roy Bean holding court down there. The skunk hanged a buddy of mine two years back for no good reason.'

The murmur of accord was cut short when Utah Gillick arrived in a lathered sweat. He had ridden hard all the way from Uvalde to deliver his mind-blowing report. Without knocking, he stumbled into the room panting heavily, much to Steiger's annoyance. 'Ain't you learned by now, Gillick? You always knock before entering my private domain. What's so darned important?'

'It's Jaybird land,' the overwrought

messenger blurted out.

'What about it?'

The cowpoke paused to draw breath before answering. 'There's a gold mine and it must have been discovered on his land.'

For a brief moment, nobody spoke. Mouths fell open, eyes popped out on stalks: gold on Jaybird land. It was barely credible. The blood drained from Steiger's face. The white worm writhed in anguish. But it was Squint Rizzo whose devious brain cottoned on to the truth immediately. He stepped forward to confront the stricken vigilante leader.

'Why, you double-crossing louse,' he railed angrily. 'Now I see it all: the reason you were so desperate to acquire farm-land that was of little use to a ranching enterprise. You'd discovered the gold and were planning to throw us poor saps to the wolves before disappearing with all the loot.' A pistol appeared suddenly in Rizzo's hand. The ominous double snap to full cock spoke volumes.

His very existence now in jeopardy,

Steiger protested his innocence of any skulduggery quickly. 'Sure, there's gold up there. And I was gonna share it out with you all once we'd taken over the valley.'

But the shifty look and the sweat-coated brow did not match the denial. Rizzo was not convinced. 'What do you say to that, boys?' he shouted, brandishing the gun with menacing intent. 'Is our noble, good-hearted boss telling the truth? Or is it all just a load of hogwash to save his miserable hide?'

Angry mutterings of discontent gave him his answer. None of those present had any doubts that Web Steiger was a ruthless go-getter who would ride rough-shod over anybody to get his own way. 'So, what's the verdict, gentlemen of the jury, is this skunk guilty or not guilty?'

A resounding verdict of *guilty* echoed around the room, bouncing off the walls and slapping the defendant in the face.

'So, Mister Webley Steiger,' Rizzo intoned, thoroughly enjoying his position as judge and executioner. 'You have been found guilty of grand theft by your peers.'

'You can't do this,' the accused man remonstrated, struggling to retain some measure of dignity. 'I ain't done nothing wrong.'

'The jury says you have,' Rizzo snapped. 'The verdict is that you're nought but a dirty, cheating rat.' An icy glower pinned down the object of his wrath. 'There's only one way to deal with scum like that.'

The gun blasted twice, an ear-splitting roar in the confined space. Steiger's punctured body slammed back with the force of the .44 shells drilling into him. He stood no chance. Before the noise and smoke had dissipated, Rizzo stepped back, facing the small gathering. His gun wavered not a jot. 'Now that this swindling chiseller has taken an early retirement, I'm taking over.' A demonic grin challenged Laredo, Buckshot Roberts and the others to contest his claim.

Nobody was eager to go up against the hard-bitten gunman who had just carried out the letter of vigilante law with its gruesome aftermath. 'A wise decision, boys. We'll ride over to the Jaybird tomorrow and take a look at our new gold mine. If'n what Utah has said is true, we're all gonna be rich.' He moved round the desk, tipping the previous incumbent onto the floor unceremoniously, and sat down. 'Fits me to a tee, don't you think?' he muttered gleefully.

'He shouldn't have held out on us, that's for sure,'

Laredo concurred, eager to show his loyalty to the new leader of the pack.

'That he shouldn't,' Rizzo agreed. A scornful glance at the bloody corpse followed. 'This skunk was ready for stepping down anyways. I just gave him a helpful nudge.' Ribald guffaws saw him picking up the crystal glass of abandoned whisky and slinging it down his throat. 'Creedy, you and Buckshot get rid of this ugly mess. Throw him down the ravine out back. Give the coyotes an early dinner.'

The two designated lackeys were not slow to obey the new boss. 'After you've done that, spread the word around that the S Bar 7 is under new management.' Squint then leaned back in the expensive leather swivel chair and puffed on the cigar. He could barely credit how fortune had suddenly swung in his favour. With Chisum and Redleg out of the way, and now Steiger, that left Squint Rizzo as top dog.

Once he had had time to assess his new position, Rizzo was well aware that with the original owners of Jaybird land now dead, he needed to claim right of tenure quickly by having an official document drawn up. And that meant a trip to Del Rio.

His next order was for Laredo, who was quickly positioning himself as the new boss's second-in-command. 'Gather a half-dozen of the boys together and get an early night's sleep. First thing in the morning, we ride for Del Rio to have this good fortune of our'n made legal. Then we head straight for the Jaybird.' His blunt-edged gaze narrowed, the tone of his voice dropping to a sibilant grunt. 'Whatever happens, that gold sure ain't going to fall into anyone else's lap. If'n the law don't back our claim, then this will.' He drew his pistol to emphasize the manner by which vigilante law would continue to operate in the Nueces Valley. Nothing had changed in that respect.

14

A Shock for Rizzo

Early next morning, Laredo was gathering his men together for the ride to Del Rio. Outside the bunkhouse, the jangle of saddle tack was overshadowed by chatter dominated by the gold discovery. Each of the men was describing how he would spend his share of the paydirt. The mood was buoyant.

'Just think of all those high class dames we can dally with,' remarked a dreamy-eyed Bug Pincher while fastening his cinch strap.

'Ain't no smart-ass gal gonna take your dough until you've had a bath,' Foxy Janus guffawed. The others joined in with the hilarity. Pincher merely shrugged his narrow shoulders. 'You fellas are just jealous of my good looks.'

'With the look of jackass, you'd be more welcome in a stable, Bug,' added Shotgun Roberts. And so the good-hearted joshing continued.

It was a shout from Creedy that saw his comrades gathering round. The owl-hoot had just commandeered the weekly news-sheet that he had found stuck in the mailbox at the entrance to the ranch. 'Take a look at this, you guys.' A jabbing finger pointed out the boldly typed advert, contained within a thick black border so as not to be overlooked. Not the smartest of jaspers, he queried puzzlingly, 'What do you reckon that's all about?'

As leading hand, Laredo snatched the sheet and read it quickly. Beetled eyebrows lifted in shocked amazement. Blue Creek Chisum alive and hiring on men! His mind spun trying to comprehend the gravity of what this intimated. Abruptly deflated, he knew that Rizzo would have to be told, and that was down to him. Promotion suddenly didn't seem such a good move.

All the others looked to him. 'That'll sure wipe the smile off Rizzo's face,' Roberts declared, clearly relieved that he was not the one having to convey such dire tidings. 'Best get it over with, Laredo.'

Reluctantly, the new deputy dragged his leaden feet towards the house. He was figuring out how to pass on the bad news quickly. 'Everything ready out there?' Rizzo barked out while strapping on his gun belt. He was thoroughly enjoying his new role as a big shot. 'We need to get on the trail pronto.'

Laredo's hesitation was quickly noted. 'Some'n bothering you?'

'Best read this first, boss,' he said nervously handing over the paper. 'Guess it changes everything.'

'What in blue blazes are you griping about?' Rizzo growled snatching the sheet. There was no reply, and no need for one as the awful truth hit home with a vengeance. 'Goldarn it! That guy was more lives than a blamed cat. What do I have to do to get rid of the varmint?' He stamped about the room. Grabbing a full bottle of whisky, he hurled it at the wall. It shattered in myriad pieces, slivers of glass and liquid flying around, but did nothing to curb his anger.

Laredo backed off, remaining silent and praying to avoid any blame. 'Don't shoot the messenger' was an adage that he now clung to desperately. But Squint Rizzo was already sussing out the implications of what the advert put forward: namely that Chisum had survived the fire. So whose body had they found burnt to a cinder in the ashes? It had to be Curly Bill Redleg. His whole body stiffened, fists bunched, knuckles white as snow.

His old pard must have sneaked out the back way and stumbled on the hidden gold mine in the cliffs behind the cabin. It all added up. But there was one mystery that still needed a solution. Who had they seen on that wagon heading off to get supplies? His brow furrowed in thought. Only one jigger it could be. Since the fistfight in Uvalde and his mysterious disappearance, nothing had been seen of the Gump. Ordway must have joined forces with Chisum, and now they were seeking to recruit a small army of labourers to protect the Jaybird from any takeover. Once again, he peered down at the advert. 'Ten o'clock, it says here,' he muttered to himself. He looked at the clock ticking away the seconds on the wall. 'Are the boys ready to ride?' he snapped to Laredo.

'Just give the word, boss, and we're ready,' he effused, eager to please the unpredictable gunman.

'I need every man on the ranch armed and ready for a set-to, including the cook and handyman,' Rizzo ordered. 'We can reach Uvalde before the deadline if'n we set off in ten minutes.' A caustic glint held the hovering lackey in a potent grip. 'And not a minute later, savvy?'

'You got it, boss,' Laredo confirmed, glued to the spot.

'Then shift your ass, dummy!'

★   ★   ★

The atmosphere in Uvalde was tense, thick enough to almost taste. Much as the council had tried to keep the upcoming showdown under wraps, such momentous tidings were bound to leak out. Those not involved had made sure to be locked up safe inside their homes. And there they sat, watching the clock circling around the dial remorselessly.

Nobody was under any illusions that the vigilantes would try to disrupt the enlistment of workers. Ben had taken charge, instructing Mayor Crawley to plant those sharpshooters he had engaged in the best places to trap the gang. 'We need to have them in position by nine o'clock,' he advised. 'Steiger will want to arrive before the recruiting drive begins, and we need to be ready for any stunt he pulls.'

He had commandeered a table from the local diner and placed it on one side of the street, facing the direction from which he expected the vigilantes to appear. There he sat on a chair, checking his guns and with a pencil and enrolment sheet ready.

'You can't face these jaspers alone,' Crawley protested. 'Let me stand alongside you. I'm the mayor of this town and it's my duty to prove I have the guts to make a stand when the chips are down.'

Crawley's stoic determination to lend his support was touching, and Ben hadn't the heart to refuse. He accepted the offer reluctantly with a firm handshake, but also with a warning corollary. 'But when the shooting starts, which it surely will, remember that I'm a gunfighter used to this kind of shindig, and you're a blacksmith. So keep your head down and don't take any unnecessary risks.'

Ben hooked out his Hunter pocket watch. It read ten after nine. 'Go make a final check that all the men are in position. And spread the word that nobody fires a shot before Steiger pulls his gun. Then it's survival of the fittest. And that'll be us. I guarantee it.'

An easygoing smile projected total confidence. Yet inside the hero of Blue Creek was silently praying for a miracle. He was under no illusions that Steiger would arrive with a strong force of hardened gunslingers desperate to squash his philanthropic ambitions. The mayor accepted Ben's optimism at face value and proceeded on his way; he shooed kids off the street and ensured that everyone knew to keep their heads down once the fireworks erupted.

The church clock had just rung the half hour toll when riders appeared at the top end of the street. Rizzo drew his men to a halt. 'Looks mighty quiet,' he pondered nudging forward at a slow walk. 'Where is everybody?'

'Feels kind of spooky,' remarked Pincher throwing nervous glances at the blank windows that stared back oozing menace. 'I don't like it.'

'Cut the griping,' rasped the new leader, sensing the edginess taking a hold of his men. 'Just keep your eyes open for that slippery varmint, Chisum.' The object of his wrath was out of sight due to a kink in the street.

Moments later, it was Laredo who spotted him sitting behind a large table, casually studying a thick, open ledger all ready to enrol his hired hands. 'There he is,' exclaimed the tough. 'And all on his ownsome. Looks like we've arrived before anyone else has signed on.'

Gritting his teeth, Rizzo led the way up the street, stopping some twenty feet short of the centrally placed table.

Ben was frowning, unsure whether the gang leader had pulled a fast one and split his force. 'I don't see Steiger. He scared to face me?'

'Web decided it was time to take early retirement.' Rizzo chuckled. 'Or, more to the point, I decided he was no longer fit enough to run the S Bar 7. So it's me you're dealing with now, buster.'

Ben responded with a casual nod. 'Guess he was getting a bit long in the tooth. You boys ready to sign up and work for the Jaybird? I'll be paying good wages.'

The mordant smirk elicited a snarl of irritation from his nemesis. 'Don't get cocky with me, Blue Creek,' Rizzo growled. 'We both know why I'm here. You escaped from that blaze. But I'm taking over the Jaybird. And you can bet it won't be for no crop harvesting. That gold is mine.'

'Don't matter none. You're too late anyway.' Ben's rejoinder was accompanied by a casual shrug. 'I've already hired twenty guys who are down there at this minute gathering in the crops. You ain't going nowhere, except to jail, or hell — your choice.'

'And who's gonna stop me and my boys riding you down, then showing those lunkheads who's in charge now?'

The arrogant grimace was removed by Ben's following remark. 'The whole town is tired of you and your brand of vigilante law lording it over them. That gold is going to benefit the Nueces Valley, and not Squint Rizzo. Better you surrender now or face the consequences.'

'And what might they be?'

Ben pointed to the rooftops overlooking the tense confrontation. One by one, men revealed their presence, aiming rifles down at the bunching S Bar 7 hands. 'You're surrounded by people sick of being ground underfoot. One signal from me, and they'll open fire.'

Nervous looks passed between the vigilantes. This was not how it was meant to be. Already, Foxy Janus and Bug Pincher were considering throwing in the towel. But they were given no chance to capitulate. Rizzo had sworn to chop this guy down to size. And he was not giving up the chance of acquiring his very own gold mine without a fight. Submission was out of the question.

'Let 'em have it, boys,' he yelled out, drawing his revolver.

Ben kicked over the table immediately and sheltered behind it as bullets chewed lumps out of the wood. The commencement of shooting galvanized the watching townsfolk into action. Rifle fire poured down on the milling horsemen. Two were struck down immediately. The others leapt off their horses and sought cover, but there was none to be had. Earlier, Ben had ordered any means of cover to be removed from the street, foreseeing the outcome of this showdown.

The attackers put up a brief, yet

spirited resistance, but they were out-manned and outgunned. Seeing their buddies being cut down ruthlessly, the remainder decided that a plot on Boot Hill was too premature. Surrender was the only option. Guns were tossed away and hands rose.

'Don't shoot, we give up!' The fearful shout of submission came from Laredo. A raised hand, waving a muddy white bandana frantically, was acknowledged by Ben.

'Hold your fire, boys,' he ordered. 'Looks like these jaspers have had enough. But keep your eyes peeled for any false moves.'

Within half a minute of the battle erupting, it was all over. Smoke from a host of small arms and rifles drifted in the air.

'You fellas keep those hands stiff and high,' Ben rapped out carefully, showing himself, his own gun ready to deliver a hot reply to any shifty wiles. 'Any tricks and the curtain comes down.' Now that the battle was over, Obediah Crawley emerged from the blacksmith's shop, together with a host of other armed citizens.

They surrounded the miscreants and began herding them down the centre of the street. Ben watched them carefully. 'Well done, boys,' he praised the defenders. 'This is what happens when folks stick together. Anybody injured?'

'Thanks to you, Mister Chisum, not a single one of our boys was hit,' replied the bubbling Mayor. 'It was our lucky day when you came to the Nueces.'

Ben accepted the acclaim with his usual nonchalant accord. It was nothing new. But all the same, it gave him a warm feeling to know he had completed a job to his own satisfaction, as well as those for whom he had been striving. But there was still something not right. A sixth sense made him hesitate.

That was moment he noticed that Rizzo was not among the living, or the dead. He hustled along to the front of the downcast group. 'I ain't seen Rizzo since he decided to throw you all to the wolves. Where's the rat skulking?' The demand for an answer was brittle and threatening. 'Come on out with, you jerks. What stunt is he trying to pull?'

The casual gratification of moments before was discarded brusquely as he grabbed the nearest vigilante by the shirt, shaking him like a dog with a bone. 'Answer me or I'll drill you where you stand.' The barrel of his gun jabbed into Bug Pincher's neck.

But it was Laredo who spoke up. He had spotted Rizzo backing off down an alley when the fracas had blow up. Only now did he cotton that the treacherous skunk had fled to save his own skin. 'I saw him duck out the firing line down an alley back yonder, leaving us guys to enjoy all the fun.' He spat into the dirt to express his disdain for the cowardly desertion. 'My reckoning is he's heading straight for the Jaybird to grab as much gold as he can carry off.'

Ben tossed Pincher aside. His brow furrowed in serious thought. He wasn't convinced by Laredo's assertion, logical as it sounded. Rizzo would know that with the raid stymied, his disappearance would be sussed quickly and a pursuit organized by his principal adversary. With Ben Chisum hot on his tail, there would be little chance of securing the gold.

The full horror of the varmint's real intentions suddenly became obvious. Securing a hostage would act as a powerful bargaining chip, and who other than Elsa Durham could offer that security? Ben would have surrendered every danged nugget of the yellow stuff if'n it would effect her safe release.

15

Winner Takes All!

'You look after these birds,' Ben instructed Crawley. 'I'm going after that pesky coyote. He's gone after Elsa and there's only Gus Ordway standing in his way.' The sombre attitude did not auger well for the simple guy's survival. 'If'n I ain't back by tomorrow noon, head straight for the Jaybird, 'cos that's where the skunk will be headed.'

Without further ado, he scurried off uptown to the livery where his horse was stabled, cursing the delay that would allow Rizzo to stretch his lead. The chase was soon afoot, Ben urging the chestnut to stretch its legs to the limit. Yet even he knew that such a frantic dash would be counterproductive. Regretfully acknowledging the need for pragmatism, he soon forced the pace down to a steady canter. A passionate compulsion urged him to dig in the spurs. But he held his nerve knowing that Rizzo was in the same position.

A forced halt at around the halfway mark was made to rest the animal at a water hole. Recent hoof prints told him that his quarry had made a similar stop and could not be far ahead. No more than two miles from the Durham holding, a single gunshot broke in on the rhythmic pounding of hoofs.

Ben's heart skipped a beat. Throwing caution to the wind, he dug deep, urging the chestnut to a frenetic gallop. When the small homestead came into view, he reined back the reckless pace, narrowed eyes searching fearfully for any movement.

A lone horse was tethered on the outskirts of the corral. It had to be Rizzo's. The rat must have sneaked up on the cabin's occupants. Moving closer, he could see a body lying on the veranda. The bright red of new blood contrasted markedly with the plain surroundings. Ben forced a tear back. Gus Ordway had paid the ultimate price trying to protect his charge.

Ben's head drooped onto his chest, but then a steely determination to avenge the heinous murder consumed his whole being: Rizzo had a lot to answer for. He must be inside the cabin, waiting on the arrival of his sworn enemy. A frontal assault would play right into his hands. In his current position, watching from a small copse some two hundred yards from the house, he remained out of sight.

So what was the best way to tackle this dilemma? A recollection leapt into his buzzing brain that offered a solution. Elsa had showed him a tunnel dug out by her father when he had first built the cabin. Its purpose was to afford protection in earlier times when Indian raiders made frequent incursions into the area. A trapdoor in the living room gave access to the narrow tunnel, which terminated in the barn. Elsa had mentioned the escape route as a counter to Web Steiger's threats when she refused to leave the property.

It would now provide the means to

save her and capture Squint Rizzo. That was the assumption. Now he had to put it into practice. Once the decision had been made, he circled around behind a low knoll, approaching the homestead and its adjacent buildings from the rear. There he dismounted and entered the barn through a side door. So where was that exit from the tunnel?

A search of the stalls soon uncovered the trapdoor beneath a pile of hay in the one nearest the house. Ben peeped out of a dirty window. The house was no more than twenty yards away. He could see movement inside. His fists bunched, an angry snarl hissing through gritted teeth. Raised voices told him that Elsa was not submitting without a fight. But the frenzied tirade was instantly cut short.

Ben feared the worst. The blood froze in his veins. The girl was a tough cookie, but a sadistic bastard like Squint Rizzo would enjoy squeezing hard to release the fear. She was a woman alone, only able to absorb so much pressure.

Quickly, he levered up the trap, revealing a ladder disappearing into total darkness. A lamp hanging on a nail for just such an occasion as this was lit. Gingerly, he lowered himself into the dark pit. Ground level was about ten feet below. The lamp was held in front as he moved as swiftly as practicable along the narrow passage. Voices ahead warned him of the imminent arrival at the chamber beneath the living room.

Setting down the lamp on a table, he checked the Colt revolver was fully loaded, then crept up the ladder silently. This was the critical moment. He needed to catch Rizzo unawares but without putting Elsa in danger. Now the moment had arrived, he realized there were a whole heap of glitches that could go wrong. Here he was, feet away from his sworn foe, but impotent to effect a defeat as matters stood.

He hesitated, knowing that some kind of move would have to be made. Sucking in a lungful of stale air, he attempted to lift the hinged flap gingerly. If'n Rizzo spotted the movement, he was done for. But it wouldn't shift. The scraping immediately above his head was enough to tell him that somebody was sitting on a chair. He cursed under his breath. There could be no way forward until the sitter got up. All he could do now was wait and pray for yet another miracle.

Minutes that seemed like hours passed. Then a gruff voice spat out. 'What's keeping that critter? He should be here by now.' Ben sensed it had come from somewhere over by the window. Rizzo must be keeping a sharp eye open for his arrival. That meant Elsa was in the chair.

Here was his one chance to attract her attention. The tap on the floorboard was loud enough to have caught Rizzo's attention. 'What was that?' he rapped.

Elsa had likewise heard it and cottoned on to the fact immediately that somebody was in the underground cellar. She stood up, giving the impression it was her shifting the chair aside. 'I'm going to make a pot of coffee,' she said, coughing to hide the nervous inflection in her voice.

'Add a hefty shot of that moonshine your old man made,' came back the snappy reply. 'I could do with a proper drink waiting here for that skunk to turn up.'

The soft padding of feet told Ben that Elsa had gone over to the far side of the room where the cooking range was located. Here was his chance. Again, he lifted the flap, praying that the hinges had been greased. Silently, it lifted a couple of inches. Ben peered through the gap. There, exactly where he had predicted, Squint Rizzo stood, looking out of the window with a gun in hand.

This was the moment of truth. Ben knew he would only get one chance to nail the critter. Girding himself for the fray, he pushed the flap hard, coming up another couple of steps to bring his own revolver to bear. Unfortunately, one of the chair legs was still over the trap; a grinding clatter and it toppled over. Rizzo swung round, his mouth dropping open on seeing Ben Chisum rising from the bowels of the earth like some primeval denizen.

Instinct for survival kicked in. The gun swung, a thumb clawing back the hammer. Both men fired at once. The noise inside the room was deafening. Elsa's scream was automatic. She dropped the coffee pot. Both bullets dug chunks out of the woodwork, neither having found its mark. Ben let the flap drop back as another bullet thudded into the floor inches from his head.

Seconds later, he threw up the flap again, keeping his head below floor level. But Rizzo had already fled the house. Ben checked quickly that Elsa was unhurt, then dashed over to the main door of the house. He peered round the side, only to see Rizzo mounting up and riding off in the direction of the Jaybird. 'The rat figures he can still grab that gold,' he called back to Elsa. 'I'm going after him.'

Elsa hurried across. 'You be careful. That guy is pure poison.' She kissed him on the lips. 'I don't want to be running this place on my own.'

Ben's heart leapt. 'Don't worry none,

219

honey,' he waxed spiritedly. 'I'll be back with that turkey — dead or alive. It'll be his choice. Then we can run it together.'

As he rushed off to get his horse, Elsa called after him. 'Rizzo has taken the regular trail. Head straight across the north pasture and you'll cut him off at Morgan's Crossing. Aim for Stovepipe Butte. You can't miss it.'

He waved an acknowledgement of the valuable pointer, hustling round to the barn. Moments later, he emerged at a gallop. Elsa watched as he raced across the field of ripening corn, scoring a pathway through the golden crop. Cresting the ridge ahead, he spotted the prominent landmark immediately, some five miles away as the crow flies, but of Squint Rizzo there was no sign. Ben concentrated on keeping the Stovepipe in sight as he was forced to detour around boulders and through clumps of thick undergrowth.

With a deep sigh of relief, he eventually swung round a rocky outcrop, and there was the landmark beside the narrow creek known as Morgan's Crossing. This was where he joined the main trail. He could only hope that the short-cut suggested by Elsa had given him the chance to stop the fleeing brigand. Drawing his rifle, Ben settled down to wait. He had no intention of laying an ambush. Such tactics were abhorrent to his nature. Ben Chisum had always been a face-on, frontal kind of guy.

After ten minutes of waiting on ten-terhooks, the regular pounding of hoofs pricked up his ears. Legs akimbo and clutching the Winchester across his chest, he positioned himself in the middle of the trail. A plume of dust heralded the arrival of his treacherous old buddy. Rizzo spotted the motionless figure blocking his onward path immediately. He dragged the horse to a stop some twenty yards short.

The surprise at having been outman-oeuvred was evident on the twisted maw. But Squint Rizzo had not been able to survive and prosper as a hired gunman without fostering nerves of steel. 'So, it's come down to this, Blue Creek,' he remarked in a nonchalant tone that accepted the inevitability of this confrontation. 'Guess I always knew deep down it couldn't end any other way.' Slowly, he stepped down off his horse and walked towards the statuesque effigy.

Only then did Ben make a move. 'You brought it on yourself, Squint, by shopping me to the federales.' He placed his rifle on the floor. This was going to be a straight shootout — winner takes all! 'Surely you never expected me to lie down and accept such a betrayal like some whipped cur.' The gun rig was settled on his hip comfortably.

Rizzo shrugged. 'Guess I did do the wrong thing. I could always apologize and we could always shake hands. There must be enough gold in that mine for us both to live happy lives.'

'Too late for that, old buddy,' Ben disputed, shaking his head. 'Too much blood has been spilled. And, truth be told, I could never trust you again. Only one of us is gonna walk away from this.

Reckon its time to set the record straight.'

Rizzo nodded. 'How we gonna play this, then?'

Ben gestured to a prairie dog watching the intruders idly. 'That fella will soon get tired of eyeballing us. When he disappears, we get to shooting. Agreed?'

'You always did enjoy a flourish when some gun-happy kid tried to take away that reputation.' Rizzo's smile resembled that of a trapped sidewinder. 'When you're ready, old pal.'

'Don't forget, Squint, to take me down you'll need to aim dead centre. Only a heart shot will win the day,' he added in a coolly calculating voice.

Both men settled down, each with an eye on the gopher, the other on his adversary. Sure enough, after a long minute, the bored creature scooted back down its hole. Both men slapped leather simultaneously.

But Rizzo had forgotten the little trick that his counterpart effected to give him the edge: a slight leaning to the right as he drew his revolver. Rizzo was the faster but had aimed dead centre, as advised. The bullet whistled past Ben's left ear. He could feel the burn of its passing. His own bullet was more accurately placed.

Rizzo staggered back. His legs gave way. One final effort to raise his gun hand failed. Ben walked across, his own firearm never wavering. 'Guess I . . . should have . . . known you'd pull . . . that stunt. Fool me . . . for ignoring the . . . obvious.'

And with that, the gunman hit the high trail to face his own demons in the bottomless pit. Ben wasted no time contemplating idly what might have been. Squint Rizzo had paid his dues. He slung the body over his horse, then made his way back to the Durham spread slowly, using the regular trail.

Even when he was still upwards of a mile off, he could see the sylphlike form of Elsa Durham still standing on the veranda, awaiting his return. She did not appear to have moved since he departed on his vengeful mission. He waved. The gesture was returned instantly.

A feeling of euphoria washed over the hired gunfighter. His mission was complete and he had unearthed a new life, one in which the hiring of a gun played no part. And with the woman of his dreams by his side, how could such a life ever be surpassed?

Other titles in the
Linford Western Library:

REVENGE AT POWDER RIVER

John McNally

Sam Heggarty returns home to hunt for the gunmen who robbed and executed his father. As he makes his way back, he witnesses another murder and stumbles across a clue to the people responsible for his father's death. He discovers that the one person who may hold the key to the identity of his father's murderers is someone that everyone else is intent on killing. Heggarty will have to save the life of a man involved in his father's death . . .